An unexpected start of
a life-altering journey.

THE

LETTER

An unexpected start of
a life-altering journey.

THE

LETTER

From the Editors
Of *True Story* And
True Confessions

Published by True Renditions, LLC

True Renditions, LLC
105 E. 34th Street, Suite 141
New York, NY 10016

ISBN: 978-1-938877-73-5

Visit us on the web at www.truerenditionsllc.com.

Chapter 1

Grandma Hatcher's handwriting caught me by surprise. It had been over four years since I left the old house in the hills of Tennessee where she raised me. Yet, as I stared at the letter she sent by certified mail, all it took was the sight of her wavering penmanship to transform fading memories into crisp visions that tortured my heart.

"What could you want with me after all of this time?" I mumbled, tearing open the seal on the envelope with hands that tried not to tremble. The stationary she used even smelled of her lavender perfume. It reminded me of being a child again, wrapped inside her arms where everything felt safe and warm. Where her love was all I needed to make all of my hurts go away. Why did that ever have to change?

Dear Annie,

I've kept my promise and stayed out of your life since you left Claxton on your eighteenth birthday. Not because I wanted to, God knows. But, because of the look in your eye when you said that was what you wanted. I knew you meant it from the bottom of your heart, even though it was for all the wrong reasons. You thought I stopped loving you and couldn't forgive your mistakes. You thought I resented you like I did your mother. I let you believe that because it was easier than telling you the truth. I should've, long ago, but I always found a reason to wait.

Time is running out now. I'm sick and know I'm dying. I can't take these secrets to my grave and ever find peace in the hereafter. Please, come home. One more time. I can't pass on with this between us. You may never forgive me once you learn what I've done, but maybe once the truth is out, I can finally forgive myself.

I'll keep the kettle on.

Love,

Grandma Hatcher

The kettle. It whistled on the back burner of her rusted yellow gas stove like a train rushing down the track every time the water boiled for her afternoon tea. Lord, did she really still have that old thing? Then her words settled in and my chest felt weighted suddenly. She's sick? She's dying? She doesn't have much time? She doesn't want to pass on with this secret between us? It was too much to fathom. I had to sit down.

Maybe I blocked her from my life when I left that fateful day, but in my heart I always knew she was out there mulling around in that old house on Shawnee Drive. Probably dozing off in her tufted easy chair while watching her favorite soap operas or lovingly tending to her houseplants while humming softly to herself, but she was there. Like a shadow hanging in the background. A shadow I never thought would disappear.

Tears stung my eyes as I gazed at her pale blue writing paper. I was torn between years of stubborn bitterness and a new, softer feeling of regret. I couldn't imagine what kind of a secret she was talking about. What could be so dirty and horrible that it had to be revealed before she died? The tears fell from my lashes as I blinked in disbelief. It didn't matter about any stupid secret or the old grudges that lie between us, just that her life was coming to an end and it was her last request to have me come back.

"I'll be there, Gram," I whispered. "Just hang on. . . . I'm coming home."

Chapter 2

I arrived in Claxton late the following afternoon. After making arrangements at work for Mandy to take over my pre-school class and asking the neighbors to gather my mail and feed Jazzy, my cat, I drove eight hours from Ohio to the familiar neighborhood that I'd tried so hard to forget. It was odd that after so much time the place could still look the same, but the post office was still there, the little park with the benches and the fountain, even the shops along Briar Street still bustled as usual. The only thing that had changed was the little restaurant on the corner where Grandma Hatcher and I used to have chicken pot pie every Wednesday. It was now dark and vacant, with a real estate sign posted by the front door. I stared in the windows at nothing but emptiness as I slowly drove by.

Within five minutes I was signaling to turn left onto Shawnee Drive. Already I was rehearsing what I would do once I saw her again. I drove down the curbed street where I was raised until the old, two-story gray house with the peeling white shutters loomed like a ghost on my right.

At first, I imagined my blue bike with the basket on the handlebars leaning against the garage door and rows of colorful clothes flapping like flags on the clothesline in the backyard. That was how it always looked, but this time neither image was there. All I saw was an unfamiliar car parked behind Grandma Hatcher's ancient one. Uneasily, I rolled to a stop in the driveway and switched my ignition off. In the sudden silence, my heartbeat thumped like a drum.

"Annie?"

My older brother bolted through the front door with his wife and twin sons following behind him. They weren't the toddlers I remembered them as, but now were lanky young boys with expressions of mischief.

"My God," I gasped, flinging my arms out to hug him. "Brian! I can't believe it. What are you doing here?"

Suzanne briefly kissed my cheek while the boys stood silent and awkward. Brian waited several moments before attempting to answer my question. "I came as soon as I heard," he said. "I guess Dr. Schaeffer contacted you, too?"

My mind whirled like a cyclone with no direction. "Dr. Schaeffer? I don't know a Dr. Schaeffer. And you came as soon as you heard what?"

He was really speechless now, so Suzanne filled in the blanks for him as she batted mournful eyes. "We just assumed you knew when we looked out the window and saw that you made the trip. Forgive us, Annie. I guess this will come as quite a shock, but Grandma Hatcher passed away last night. We were going to contact you after we arranged for a funeral."

"That can't be," I insisted, scanning the front porch with an eager gaze as if expecting her to suddenly appear. "I just got a letter from her yesterday. She said she was sick and needed me to come home. I got here as fast as I could."

Brian shook his head and slid an arm around one of his sons. "Dr. Schaeffer called before dawn this morning and said that a neighbor had responded in concern when there were no lights in Grandma Hatcher's house last night even though her car was in the driveway. When the police came to follow up, they found that she'd passed away in her chair with a Bible on her lap. I know how much comfort she found in those pages and only hope that helped to ease her final moments."

I began to shake uncontrollably and hugged my arms around my waist. "I didn't even know she was sick. I hadn't heard from her for the last four years, but yesterday I got a certified letter from her saying she had something to tell me. That she was dying and wanted to share some kind of horrible secret before going to her grave. I thought of calling her to tell her that I was going to make arrangements at work and then be on my way, but I was afraid to speak to her after all of this time. I figured I'd just wait until today and see her in person. I never thought . . . I mean, I didn't expect. . . ."

One of Brian's boys' lips, colored with what looked like fruit punch, twitched. "Can we go inside now? I want to watch TV."

His interruption made Suzanne sadly smile. "I'm sorry, Josh. I know all this grown-up stuff is hard for you and Trevor to be patient with, but this is your Aunt Annie, and we haven't seen her in a very long time. Go on inside and turn on the TV. We'll be coming in soon ourselves."

Trevor stared at me when he saw my tears. "It's okay, Aunt Annie. Don't worry. Grandma Hatcher is in Heaven now. That's where my hamster went, and I know it's a nice place because that's what everyone says."

My heart melted as I looked down at his innocent face. "That's true, sweetheart. Thank you for reminding me."

Satisfied that he helped, Trevor ran to catch up with his brother who already had his foot in the front door. I watched them until they disappeared into the house and had to force my eyes back to Brian's.

"He may be just six, but I think what he said was true," my brother said, reaching out for my hand. "She's in a better place now and we have to hang on to that. The cancer was slowly eating away at her, but now she isn't suffering anymore."

I wanted to remind him what she wrote to me. That she was very despondent over some sort of secret, but Suzanne already eased her arm around me and nudged me toward the house.

"We'll have some tea," she said. "I'm sure there's some of Gram's favorite orange and spice tea bags in the canister by the stove. That should make us all feel better. She would've wanted us to do that, I think."

I'll keep the kettle on. . . . I can't take this secret to the grave. . . . Come home, Annie, I've got something to tell you. Come home, I'll keep the kettle on. . . .

My flesh shivered with something I couldn't identify. "Yes, Suzanne. I know you're right. She would've wanted us to have tea."

Chapter 3

Everything was as I remembered it. The braided rugs on the hardwood floors, the brass lamps with the yellowed shades, the brown sofa with the embroidered throw pillows, and the grandfather clock in the corner of the living room. I could barely even glance at the deserted easy chair where Brian said Grandma died with a Bible on her lap. She loved that chair and often nodded off while she was sitting there. I used to cover her with an afghan and leave her there to nap.

So much was familiar, as if time simply stood still. The place even smelled the same. Kind of like a combination of lemon furniture polish and mothballs. All that was missing was Grandma Hatcher herself, enjoying having a house filled with guests and wanting to fix them something to eat.

The boys sat on the couch hypnotized by a cartoon on the television, while Brian and Suzanne led the way to the kitchen. Tears welled in my eyes at the sight of her china teacup with the little chip in the rim turned upside down in the dish drain. She always put it there after rinsing it out. I must've seen her do that a million times. The delicate, little red roses painted on the side brought back memories of the soft blush in her cheeks.

"Here, Annie," Brian said, sliding out one of the chairs at the table. "Sit down. We'll fix the tea."

"It's just so hard," I managed to say, settling into my seat and gazing at the room around me. "Being back here, I mean. It's been a long time."

Suzanne filled the kettle with water and lit the back burner as Brian gathered some cups and checked the canister for tea bags. Orange and Spice. Grandma Hatcher's forever favorite. I never saw her even try another kind.

"How's things in Columbus?" Suzanne asked, forcing her voice to sound light. "The last time you wrote, you said you were thinking of buying a larger apartment. I'd imagine that means your teaching job is paying well."

My attention traveled to the fridge where papers were arranged on the door with plastic fruit magnets. It looked like a grocery list and some photos of the twins along with magazine clippings that must've meant something to her. She was always reading anything she could get her hands on.

"Work is fine," I answered, hating how numb I was feeling. "I just decided not to move. It's too much of a bother. The place I have is really comfortable enough, anyway."

"I wasn't surprised when you said you were promoted to Assistant Director," Brian said, smiling. "You've always had a way with kids, and you're probably a real asset to that pre-school."

Suzanne nodded. "We've often said what a good mother you're going to make one day. I know Brian keeps hoping you'll meet a nice young man and. . . ."

The water began boiling and the teapot screamed out a whistle. For a moment, I saw Grandma Hatcher hustling to the stove, telling the kettle that she was coming, as if it had ears of its own. I began to tremble again and lost track of everything we were talking about. Something cold kept feathering over my skin.

"She was going to tell me something," I said with concern. "Something so important that she said she wouldn't rest in her grave unless I knew the truth. What could've been so bad that she would've kept it from me all of these years? What kind of a secret would have been so torturous for her to keep?"

My brother and his wife exchanged baffled glances. "I don't know," Brian said, handing me my tea before sitting at the table with his own. "We always came to visit nearly every Sunday and she never once said anything about a secret to me."

"We can't imagine what it would be," Suzanne added as she joined us. "Grandma Hatcher hardly ever spoke of you at all, and when someone did mention your name, she'd kindly leave the room. Not because she wanted to, we could see, but because she had to. It was always too painful for her to endure."

My throat tightened as I dipped my gaze. The shame of the past threatened to come back and smother me. "She never forgave me for it," I said softly. "I knew she never would. That was why I left as soon as I turned eighteen. I wish we could've stayed close, but I knew she honestly resented me, just like she resented Mom. It hurt too much. We could no longer be a part of each other's lives."

Brian met my troubled gaze. "I think she forgave you, Annie. I just think she never forgot."

"Do you think I have?" I snapped back, my voice escalating. "I work with children every single day. I love what I do and it gives me great satisfaction, but seeing their little smiles and melting in their wonderful hugs only reminds me of the child I lost. Not a second goes by that I don't feel this hollow in my heart. Maybe it was a long time ago and I know I was certainly too young, but I felt my baby move inside of me. I was only a kid myself, but it changed me just the same. I loved my child. I wanted to be a mother no matter how impossible the future seemed. I knew Grandma Hatcher disapproved of my plans, but I never would've given my child up for anything. I know I could have made it if my baby didn't die at birth."

"You were only fifteen, for God's sakes." Brian flinched his jaw muscle. "How could you have taken care of yourself and a baby?"

"I would've found a way."

"Maybe so," he answered, shaking his head. "But it would've been a constant uphill climb for you. Taking care of a baby, finishing school, finding a job to support yourself and a child. It's hard enough with both a mother and a father in the picture, let alone just you handling all the responsibility. Who knows whatever happened to good old Michael? I don't know what kind of a man can live with himself after turning his back on his responsibility."

I would've insisted that I could've done it without Michael or anyone, but something in Suzanne's expression made me fall silent. She was usually composed and poised, ready with a smile, but suddenly she looked down at her lap with pained creases in her brow.

"Are you all right?" I asked, lightly touching her arm.

Her gaze lifted to Brian's and momentarily lingered there before shifting over to mine. Her eyes were cold and angry.

"I'm fine," she answered with an edge to her voice before rising up from her chair. "I just need to check on the boys."

She left the room and I stared at my brother, who shifted uncomfortably where he sat. Whatever was going on inside of his marriage, he didn't like it put on display. With a tense smile and a sudden change of topic, he got back on more stable turf.

"I think we ought to have a simple service," he stated. "Grandma Hatcher had very few close friends, and I know how she hated attention. Maybe something brief at the church up on Maple Street. She went on occasion and seemed to like it there."

"I'm sure that would be fine."

"She loved you a lot, you know. Whether you believe it or not, you were always very special in her heart."

His image blurred as my eyes filled with tears. "I disappointed her, Brian. Just like Mom did when she abandoned us and ran off to California. You were the only one out of all of us that she could be proud of. You did pretty good with your life."

Now the look that riddled Suzanne's face only a few short minutes ago was plastered on my brother's. The pain I saw there startled me.

"Brian, what is it?" My gaze narrowed as I watch him stand.

"Nothing," he grumbled, carrying his empty cup to the sink. "Let's just leave it alone."

"There's something wrong between you and Suzanne," I pressed on. "I can see it's really hurting the both of you. I'm your sister. I'd like to try and help, if I could."

He leaned on the counter and looked out the window at some

8

blackbirds balancing on a telephone wire. "Nothing can help, Annie. I'd really like to just forget it. Just don't think that I did so great with my life. I've got things I'm not proud of, too."

Just then, the front doorbell chimed. By the time we got to the foyer, Suzanne had already answered it. On the stoop was Edna Daniels, who lived in the house next door. I remembered her to be Grandma Hatcher's close friend and someone she spent time with every day. She had aged quite a bit in the four years since I'd seen her, but despite her appearance, she still had the most incredible eyes. They were kind and gentle, sparkling with a kind of contentment that I had always hungered for, but never experienced. She carried a dish wrapped in foil. Her frail body was rigid and shook slightly from the effects of Parkinson's disease, yet the glow on her face was proof that she wouldn't let it break her spirit. Already I was thankful that she'd made the effort to come. I had the distinct feeling that Edna Daniels was supposed to be here.

"I don't mean to intrude at such a tender time," she said as we all gathered around the door. "I wanted to give my sympathies. I was the one who called the police last night so they would check things out. I knew something was wrong when Velma's lights weren't on and kind of suspected that the good Lord took her." She held out the covered dish as her hands tremored badly. "I wanted to help and knew that you had to eat. I made a chicken casserole. I know that's one of your favorites, Josh."

"I'd rather have pizza," Josh scoffed, looking up at his mother.

She quickly shuffled him into the background and smiled at the old woman. "He'll eat it. He just likes to be difficult. This was really so very nice of you to do, Edna."

Brian opened the door and invited her in as I watched her every move. In a way, I thought she was watching mine, too. We kept smiling and looking at each other. She ended up staying and joining us for dinner since she usually ate dinner alone. Her husband passed on over ten years ago, and her only companionship now was a very pampered parakeet.

"He can talk, you know," she said to the boys who both wore milk mustaches and picked at their casserole. "Pesky can say 'Hello' and 'Have a good day' and even 'It's time to go to bed.' He's very smart and thinks like a human. He knows how to pick the lock on his cage and let himself out. I thank God every day that we don't have a cat!"

We laughed and she seemed to love it. Bringing joy to other people was obviously something she found satisfaction in, as she looked at each one of us, studying our faces with her eyes sparkling like gemstones. I couldn't get enough of her and didn't exactly know why. I had a strange feeling that I should draw closer to her.

9

By the time she got ready to leave, the boys had forgiven her for the casserole and told her all their football stories. How Trevor was faster, but Josh a little tougher on tackles and they both wanted to play pro one day. They made her promise that they could come visit Pesky and see him talk in person. She seemed as excited about that prospect as they did.

"I'll see you tomorrow then," Edna said before going out the front doorway. "I'd like to help with the funeral plans. Maybe if it's just to make some phone calls or keep the coffee coming. Anything to feel useful so I don't miss her too much. She was a dear woman, you know. Very, very sweet. I'll miss her more than I could say."

I watched her hobble across the front porch as Brian and Suzanne went to tend to their boys. I knew I had to say something more to her before she was out of sight.

"You knew her better than anyone, didn't you?" I called out.

The woman stopped and slowly turned, shaking like a delicate leaf alone on a winter's branch. Her face was pale and badly wrinkled, but her eyes were still energetic. I found them absolutely captivating.

"Yes," she answered. "I think I did. We've been close for a very long time."

I stepped out on the porch, letting the screen door fall closed behind me. The evening air was light and cool, caressing my face as I slowly walked up to her.

"Close enough to share difficult secrets?" I asked, studying her reaction.

Her head cocked. "Why would you ask that?"

"Because of a letter I got from her yesterday. She told me she was dying and I had to come back home. That there was something horrible she'd been keeping from me for the last four years and she couldn't rest in peace until she came out with the truth."

Edna let her gaze drift off over my shoulder to the darkened sky behind me. She pondered her next words and spoke them very carefully. "Truth can be a very powerful thing, Annie. It can either heal broken lives or destroy what is left of them. There is no in between. Whoever insists upon having such truth should have an idea which way it will go for them and make sure they are prepared. I speak from experience, dear girl. This advice comes from my heart. Be sure you know what you're asking for because it could change your life once you get it. Are you sure you're ready for that?"

I stood motionless without an answer as she turned and went on her way. There was so much more I wanted to say to her and a wealth of questions I needed to ask, but what she said stopped me cold with sudden doubts I didn't have before. What if this secret was powerful enough to shatter my life and leave me stumbling through the ruins?

What if it was something terrible that I wouldn't know how to handle? I came to Claxton on a mission to accept whatever truth Grandma Hatcher had been hiding, but was I really ready for what this buried truth could be?

"I don't know," I said softly into the dark. "God help me, but I really don't know."

Brian and Suzanne rounded up the twins by nine o'clock that night. The boys were growing cranky and wanted to go home. Everyone had a long day and was tired.

"Please come with us and stay at the house," Brian said. "The guest room is very comfortable, and I know the boys would love to show you their football trophies."

Trevor yawned. "I've got more than Josh."

"Do not," Josh argued.

"Do, too, dork."

Josh turned red and lunged to punch him. Suzanne had swift reflexes and pulled the two apart, giving me a quick hug good-bye before taking them out to the car.

"Will you come with us?" Brian pleaded. "I hate to think of you here alone. We can come back tomorrow after working out the funeral arrangements and figure out what to do with her things."

I scanned the quiet living room with the grandfather clock ticking loudly in the corner. Grandma Hatcher's weathered easy chair sat like an old, abandoned friend.

"I appreciate the invitation, but I think I'm going to stay here. I kind of feel like I need time alone."

His smile was gentle. "I understand. We'll be back in the morning and discuss the plans we need to make." He hugged me close and stroked my hair. "It's good to have you home, Annie."

As soon as their car backed out of the driveway and vanished into the night, I got my suitcase out of my trunk and carried it upstairs. My footsteps slowed as I walked down the hallway, passing the bathroom, the hall closet, and then Gram's room before coming to my own, the only one with the door closed. It was harder than I expected to simply turn the knob and open it. I wasn't really sure what I would find. I didn't know if it had been changed around and redecorated or if she had left it like it was.

Chapter 4

Even if there was nothing inside and it was just a plain, empty room, the memories were still there, as if it all happened yesterday. Nothing would ever make them go away.

"Breathe, Annie. Don't hold back the pain. It'll take longer if you fight the contractions."

"I'm scared, Gram. It hurts! I don't know if I can do this."

"You don't have much of a choice, my dear girl. The head is already crowning. Grab hold of the bedposts and bear down with all of your might. Whether you think you can or think you can't, this baby is going to be born."

Swallowing my tears, I opened the door and flicked up the light switch on the wall.

She hadn't changed a thing. Everything was like I had left it—from the stuffed animals displayed on my crisply-made bed to the pile of teen magazines and scattered nail polish bottles on the top of my dresser. My gaze then wandered to the phone on the nightstand where more slivers of the past came rushing back. Whispered conversations in the middle of the night with Michael on the other end from his dorm room in Michigan.

He wanted to marry me. It would be the right thing. He'd fly back to Claxton over Christmas break and we'd do it swiftly at the courthouse. No mention of love or happily-ever-after, just that a baby was coming and he had to do right. I felt like a disease he was willing to contract or a damaged piece of furniture he was forced to accept. It was nothing like the eternal love between a husband and a wife like I'd always dreamed of. I was wrong to give my virginity to him with his being so much older and bound for college, but I thought we had something special. Something sacred.

He was the only boy who ever said he loved me. Grandma Hatcher never liked him, and I cried for days when she insisted I not see him. I tried so hard to make her understand. Michael wasn't a reckless boy that would hurt me in any way. He was mature and sensible. Strong and protective. So handsome that he set me on fire. We finally resorted to meeting secretly at night after Gram went to bed and I could slip out my bedroom window and climb down the tree to his waiting arms. It felt so right just to be with him. I prayed the news I wrote to him after he left wouldn't split us apart.

"You sound different," I remember saying only weeks after he moved away. "I'm glad you called, but it sounds like you really didn't want to."

"I do," he answered, his voice flat in a lie. "What's with the third degree?"

"I'm sorry if that's what it feels like, but I'm just worried about us, that's all. I wasn't even sure if you'd call once you got my letter. I was afraid you'd think I told you just to trap you, but that wasn't the reason at all. I did it because you deserve to know. I'm having this baby and you're the father. Whether you want to be a part of it or simply walk away, I'm going to love you forever."

"You act like I have choices. That's a little unreal, don't you think?"

"I would never force you into anything, Michael. You know me better than that."

"But I guess you don't know me if you think I could live with myself and walk away. I'll marry you, Annie. I'll do the right thing. Christmas break is coming and I'll come back home to Claxton. I guess we'll do it simple at the courthouse. That would be the fastest. We'll have to get an apartment here while I finish college, but I'll get a job and support us. I'll work seven nights a week if I have to. I'll do my part because I know I'm to blame for not using protection that night. It was dumb, that's all. I should've known it would end like this. Now, we just have to handle the responsibility we've created."

Tears streamed down my cheeks as I pressed the phone to my ear that night. I could hear him breathing, hear the TV, hear the voices of his roommate and friends in the background. I remember wanting to crawl through the wires and feel the comfort of his embrace. Some kind of warmth. Something to show me he loved me like he used to just weeks before when I gave him my virginity in the backseat of his car.

"Michael, I love you."

There was no response on the other end.

"Did you hear me? I love you. Do you still love me, too, or has my getting pregnant ruined everything between us?"

"I told you I'll do right by you. What more can I say? I've gotta go. Take care of yourself. Bye."

I shook myself back to the present and set my suitcase down. It didn't matter. Those days were all done and gone. Once I lied to him about the miscarriage, it spared us any more misery. I had too much pride to make a man marry me for any reason other than undying love. He'd never know the difference, because his family moved shortly after he left for school and mine thought he dumped me for being pregnant. It made one tidy package of untruths that worked for the best. Best for me. Best for Michael and for the child we almost had. I still wondered if God punished me by taking my baby because of all my lies.

The ringing of the phone made me jump out of my skin. I placed a hand to my heart as I gathered my breath and answered it. It was Edna, just checking up.

"I'm going to bed now and wanted to make sure you were doing all right over there. If it's too hard for you to sleep tonight, just come over and knock on my door. We'll sit up together because I'm missing her, too. I doubt there'll be much rest for either of us."

I smiled. "You're a very sweet lady, Edna. My gram was very lucky to have you as a friend. But I'm okay. It's hard, but I need to be here."

"I know you do, Annie. I think Velma would've been so happy that you came. Just remember that I'm here if you need anything."

"I just wish things were different," I explained, fearing she'd hang up. It felt easy to open up and share with her. "I always thought about coming back and seeing her again, but it seemed best the way we left things. I knew I shamed her so. I guess I thought I'd done her a favor by disappearing from her life."

"Dear Annie," she said. "You never knew just how much she loved you, did you? You were like a second chance to her. She never had much of a relationship with your mother, and it always left a void in her heart. But you, well, you were like the daughter she always wanted to love, and your relationship with her meant the world. She never would've let go of that if you didn't insist on cutting the ties. She wasn't ashamed of you, Annie. You were the light of her life. I'm sure she would've told you that had she lived long enough to see you."

I sat on the edge of my bed, fatigued and confused. "That couldn't have been the secret she was talking about. She had something else to tell me. Now I'll never know what was so important that she had to send me that letter before she died."

"If something is meant to be known, I believe it will be revealed. Just trust in God making everything right."

"You know what it is, don't you?" I asked, aching for some kind of sense to this. "She must've shared everything with you since you were such close friends."

She waited before saying anything. For a moment I thought she hung up, but I heard Pesky squawking in the background and saying it was time for bed. She chuckled, as if happy for the diversion. It swung the attention of the moment in a much lighter direction.

"He knows the routine," she said. "He knows it's way past our bedtime and he's nagging me to shut off the lights. He won't sleep unless it's all dark and I've covered his cage with a towel. Just remember what I told you. I'm right next door if you need me. Sleep well, Annie girl. Just know your gram loved you. I'll see you in the morning."

14

So much emotion was still knotted inside of me, so I decided to take a bath. It helped to relax me, but with so much on my mind, I knew I was far from being able to sleep. Warm milk usually helped, and I was going to go downstairs and see if Gram had any milk in the fridge. I wrapped my robe around myself, relishing its comfort, and made my way down the hall.

This time as I came to her bedroom, I stopped in the doorway and turned on the light. She'd gotten a new bedspread to replace the old beige one with the badly frayed edges. This one was colorful. It surprised me she had chosen something so loud. I remembered her taste as being very simple and mellow. Her reading chair was still in the corner by the window where the bookcase also stood, and the mahogany dresser. The big, oval mirror gleamed as if freshly polished. Even her crystal perfume bottles were still neatly lined up next to her tortoise shell hairbrush. I could practically see her standing there in her nightgown, running the brush through her thinning gray hair and humming contentedly to herself. Slowly, I walked around as an ache rose up in my throat. So many times we had long talks in this room on that old bedspread that she obviously had gotten rid of. Talks of school, of my mother, of why she wouldn't say yes to a dog, and most of all about the subject of boys. Grandma Hatcher was so patient and wise, listening to everything that poured out from my heart and having all the right things to say in return. She always knew how to take my troubles and make them go away, always—until I went and got myself pregnant. That was one problem she couldn't erase.

Just as I was about to turn and leave, something caught my eye—an old photo on her nightstand in a small brass frame that was never displayed there before. I came closer and saw a young Grandma Hatcher standing next to Grandpa Hatcher, who died when I was two. They had on their Sunday clothes and both wore proud, broad smiles as Gram cradled an infant in her arms.

"My God," I gasped, touching the baby's image with my fingers. "That's my mother. It has to be. She was the only child they ever had."

Grandma Hatcher never had any reminders of my mother around the house. It was strictly forbidden. She always tried to forget that my mother ever existed because she didn't respect her. She couldn't comprehend how her little girl turned out so cold. To have children and abandon them with nothing more than a note of apology was something she never forgave. Brian was older and remembered her, but I was just a baby. He said she was loud, pretty, had a lot of boyfriends, and she always wore too much perfume.

That was all I really knew about her. That, and she never loved or wanted us. Grandma Hatcher spoke of her only if we brought it up, but always said we were better off without her and that no decent, caring woman would've done the things she did. In her words, it was unforgivable for a mother to turn her back on her kids. . . . Yet, did this photo mean she did somehow come to a place of forgiveness inside her angry heart? Why else would this photo even be here? I tried to remember where she kept the family album. Seeing this made me want to look at all the photos she kept. I went to her closet and checked the top shelf before kneeling and looking under her bed. When that turned up nothing, I almost went back to concentrating on getting the warm milk, but then I noticed the album in her bookcase. The burgundy leather cover brought back memories of precious times in my childhood when we'd sit together and go through it page by page. There were always blank spots where I knew she had removed certain snapshots that I assumed were of my mother.

I wondered if the picture on the nightstand meant those blank spots were now filled. Was she somehow able to see my mother's face again and not lose herself in bitterness?

Chapter 5

To my disappointment, nothing had changed in the album. The places where certain photos once were still had nothing there. But soon I began smiling as I looked at other pictures of Brian and me when we were kids. One showed us unwrapping Christmas presents under a glowing tree and another had us eating melting ice cream cones on the front porch in the heat of summer. Happy times that I once cherished until they got smothered by all the wrongs I'd done. Funny how the pain of a few years can wipe out the joy of a whole lifetime. It got too hard to look at and I went to put the album away, but as I did something slipped out from the pages and drifted down to the floor. It was an envelope, yellowed with age, addressed to Velma Hatcher, and postmarked twenty years ago. The penmanship was graceful and slanted. My curiosity was piqued.

Hesitating, I unfolded the letter and the room whirled around me as I read it. It was from my mother and she was asking to come home.

I can't undo the past or make up for what I took from the children. All I can promise you is that I'm a different person now than I was when I walked away. I've learned the difference between what's important and what only leaves you empty. It took me a long time, but I've truly changed.

I want to come home and try to explain things to Brian and Annie. At the same time, I don't want to disrupt their lives or do anything that might hurt them any more. I know you've given them the love and care that I wasn't able to give in the past and you've made their lives secure. For that, I owe you more than my life, so only with your permission will I return to Claxton. Only if you feel they could accept me back after all that I've done. I dream only of holding them again and telling them that their mommy does love them.

I'll wait to hear from you. If you don't write back, I'll know it's too late and respect the fact that you think Annie and Brian are better off without me. It will break my heart, but I know that's probably what I deserve. I only hope one day you can all forgive me.

Love,
Dorothy

I couldn't believe what I was holding in my hands. I read it over and over as sobs erupted, then turned into waves of anger. Twenty years ago would have meant I was only two and Brian would have been six. How could Grandma Hatcher deny our mother from coming back into our lives? All of these years I thought she didn't want us. Was this the secret she carried? She knew how to contact my mother all along and we could've been a real family!

Wiping away tears, I raced into my bedroom and got my address book from my purse. I found Brian and Suzanne's number and quickly dialed it with shaking hands. It was late and I knew I would probably wake them, but what I had just discovered couldn't wait. My brother had to know what Grandma Hatcher had kept from us.

"Hello?"

It was Suzanne. She didn't sound right, but I figured the call must have startled her.

"It's Annie, Suzanne. I'm sorry to be calling so late, but I need to speak with Brian. It's really important."

There was a long pause. "He's not here."

My eyes dashed to the clock by the phone. Where would he be at a quarter after twelve in the morning?

"Where is he?" I asked, growing very concerned.

Again, I heard nothing at first. "Brian should be the one to tell you. I really can't handle this right now."

She was crying and I was upsetting her. I wasn't sure what to do. "Are you okay, Suzanne? It sounds like you're crying. Did something happen after you left here tonight?"

"I can't say anything. It's really Brian's place to explain it."

"Talk to me," I begged. "At least tell me where my brother is so I don't worry half to death."

"He's where he's been for the last six months," she blurted out. "Living with the woman he loves."

Now I was the one who had no words. I heard what she said and knew that she meant it, but it was so outrageous it could've been a joke. If it weren't for the excruciating pain in her voice and a really bad gut feeling, I would've thought it was a prank. After all, they were high school sweethearts happily married over nine years. They were parents of two wonderful children.

"Suzanne," I gasped. "I don't understand. He didn't say anything to me about that and even invited me to stay at your house tonight."

"We agreed that our problems would stay our problems. With all that's happening with Gram's death, we didn't want to make things worse. We were going to put on a false front just so you thought things were normal. If you accepted our offer and stayed at our house, we would've played the role of a happy husband and wife while you were

18

here, telling the boys not to say anything, but he would have slept on the bedroom floor."

"I can't believe it," I said. "I could tell something was wrong between you earlier, but I had no idea it went this deep. How could he be in love with another woman? I know how much you and the boys mean to him."

"That's what I thought, too," she answered, her words trembling with heartache. "But in the end you never know a person at all. Not unless they really want you to."

It hit hard. That was a lesson I was learning all too well. "I'm sorry to put you on the spot this way. I know it must have been hard for you to tell me. What I was calling him for can wait until tomorrow when he comes over. I'm just really so very sorry."

"Annie, please don't tell him that I told you. I think it would be best if you just let him tell you on his own, if that's what he decides. As messed up as things are right now, he's still a proud man and I don't want to make things worse. Can you understand that? Will you do me that favor?"

"Of course," I assured her. "It's your private business and I won't intrude unless he needs to confide in me. You're welcome to talk to me, too, if you need to open up to someone who cares."

"Thank you, Annie. I'll remember that. God bless." With that, there was the click of our disconnection.

I laid back on my bed as my world began to fall away from me. Too much was happening. Nothing felt real anymore. Suddenly, I recalled Edna's words of warning as fresh tears rolled down my face.

Truth is a powerful thing, Annie. It can either heal broken lives or destroy what there is left of them. Are you ready? Are you ready . . . are you ready?

Chapter 6

The pale morning sun poured through my bedroom curtains. I'd watched the dark of night melt away to the light of day since sleep never came.

All I could manage was to lay in bed while my mind tangled with so many thoughts. Of Grandma Hatcher and the secret she wanted to tell me before death stole her chance, of the letter from my mother that slid out from the photo album, and of my brother and his strange betrayal to the family he loved.

It seemed my entire life had fallen apart around me in the last twenty-four hours and I didn't quite know how to cope with it. I decided to get dressed and go next door in hopes that Edna was an early riser. Her company would be soothing and she could probably even make me laugh.

If anything, I needed to see the calm in her sky blue eyes.

I rang the bell after seeing her kitchen light on. The chime must've startled Pesky, who immediately began squawking an ear-piercing hello. Soon, the door opened and Edna smiled back at me. She took my hand in hers as she ushered me in.

"I was hoping you'd come over this morning," she said, showing me to the loveseat in her living room. "I can see by the fatigue on your face that you got about as much sleep as I did. I finally gave up and started baking before dawn to try and get my mind off things. Now, I'm glad I did. We'll have some nice banana nut bread with a hot cup of tea. I'm assuming, of course, that you haven't had breakfast."

"No, actually I haven't," I answered, settling onto the sofa. "That empty house was too quiet. I needed companionship more than I needed food. After such a long night of tossing and turning, I had to get out of there for a while."

She patted my knee with her knobby hand. "You did the right thing. I'll go get us that nut bread and tea. Just stay cozy where you are and we'll have a nice visit."

"Can I help you? I don't want to put you to all this trouble."

Her smile was one of genuine pleasure, as if doting on people was a treat she rarely had. "Nonsense. It's no trouble. Just stay here and keep Pesky company. He's sizing you up from the corner over there. Maybe you two can make friends."

As she shuffled off, I glanced at the wrought iron cage where a vivid green bird with whitish crown and bib feathers was staring back at me from his perch. His head cocked from side to side as if he didn't quite know what to make of me.

"Well, hello, Pesky," I said softly, walking over to the cage. "I've heard an awful lot about you."

"Women and children only!" he answered. "Women and children only!"

Edna's laughter could be heard filtering out from the kitchen. "I watched a reenactment of the Titanic the other night and now that's his favorite thing to say. It seems like he picks up a new phrase every day. He never fails to amaze me."

I smiled into the depthless black eyes that didn't take themselves off me. "I didn't know parakeets could talk like that."

"He's a Quaker Parakeet," she called back. "They're supposed to be wonderful talkers. Pesky knows a lot of words and phrases that he's accumulated over the years."

"He's delightful," I said, now wandering toward the fireplace where a mantel of framed photos caught my attention. "He must make for good company."

"Well, after Albert passed on, it gave me someone to talk to. Some people might see me as crazy chatting away to a bird, but Pesky's been with me for nearly ten years. I consider him a real family member."

Curiously, I gazed at the row of old photographs where people in vintage clothing smiled back from a different era. The only modern picture was a color snapshot of a handsome young man leaning up against a cherry red pickup truck. His smile was a bit lopsided, but it gave him a certain charm. Edna caught me studying it as she came in the room and carefully set a tray on the coffee table.

"That's Clayton, my only grandson. Handsome as a prince, isn't he? He moved here from Philadelphia a year ago. You might get to meet him since he's the pastor of our neighborhood church now. He's a beautiful man with a heart of pure gold. He simply adored your grandmother."

"The Maple Street Church?" I asked, recalling how Brian had mentioned it. "We were thinking of having Grandma Hatcher's memorial service there."

"That would be a wonderful idea. Velma attended regularly up until her illness got to be too much. She would've been very pleased to be remembered there and have my Clayton do the eulogy. He came out to her house in the final weeks, praying with her, and keeping her strong. She called him her angel of mercy."

A wave of guilt washed over me as I went to sit back down on the couch. Tears prickled my eyes as I tried to distract myself by getting a napkin and piece of banana bread. It smelled heavenly and the tea beckoned with comfort, yet my sadness overwhelmed me like a pit that kept getting deeper. I blinked and my welling tears began to dribble down my face. I reached for another napkin and mopped at my eyes with embarrassment. Edna watched with sympathy, but didn't try to stop me. Somehow, she knew it was a process I had to go through.

"You wish you would've been here for her, don't you?" she asked. "She wouldn't want you to be so torn up about it, Annie. Despite your parting of the ways, she always loved you and knew you loved her, too. She didn't die without you in her heart."

"It was so stupid," I choked out, shedding more tears. "My dumb pride wouldn't let me pick up the phone over the years. It wouldn't let me write or even visit. I wanted to so many times, but then I'd remember how far we drifted apart after I got pregnant. I figured if she couldn't forgive my mistake, I'd just disappear like my mother did. She saw me cut from the same cloth as her, anyway. Careless. Irresponsible. A real disappointment to the family. She didn't want anything to do with her and it just made me feel like she wouldn't want anything to do with me. Now she's gone and it's too late to ever make things right. I was so stupid to keep that wall between us after all she's done for Brian and me. Maybe we could've gotten closer again if I only made some kind of an effort before it was too late."

"Regrets are poison," Edna answered, handing me my teacup and then taking a sip from her own. The Parkinson's made her hand tremble so that she almost spilled tea on herself. She carefully set the cup back on the saucer and began slicing the banana bread. "I have them. We all have them and they are as useless as a three-legged chair. It took me a long time to realize how important it is to get over the things we can't change. I know Velma would've wanted you to do that."

There was a brand of sorrow in her voice that powerfully drew me in. "You sound like you have a lot of wisdom about life and its problems. I can sense from you that you've been hurt by something in your past. I hope I'm not being too bold, but I remember you saying that you spoke from experience when you warned me that secrets can destroy a person's life. Did someone keep something from you that you later found out? Is that why you wanted me to be sure I could handle Grandma Hatcher's secret?"

The normal sparkle to her eyes faded into a cloudy stare. I noticed her gaze traveled to Clayton's photograph on the mantel. A flicker of emotion played on her face as if she were reliving memories as painful as jagged glass. Memories she wasn't comfortable sharing.

"Let's just say that I gave you that advice because I don't want to see your life shattered forever. Sometimes it isn't so bad to keep things unknown."

It wasn't that it was cold at all in the room. In fact, it was more than comfortable, yet I felt an icy chill that forced me to wrap my hands around my steaming cup. It was as if a place in the deepest part of my soul needed a warmth that nothing could give it. The silence left us both stewing in our thoughts until Pesky decided to brighten things.

"Don't shoot," he squawked. "You've got me cornered. Don't shoot!"

Our laughter took the place of the thick tension. I began to like that bird. "Where did he learn that? Don't tell me you watch police dramas on top of educational things."

Edna shrugged. "Guilty. I'm a sucker for men in uniform."

Just then, I heard the faint slamming of car doors. It was nearly nine o'clock and I knew it had to be Brian. Most likely he didn't get a whole lot of sleep, either, even if it was in his girlfriend's bed.

"That's probably my brother and his family," I said, placing my cup aside and rising. "I'd better get over there before they wonder where I went. Thank you so much for the wonderful nut bread and tea. It was really delicious."

She got to her feet and followed me toward the door. "I hope I was able to give you more than food for your stomach. I hope you take away some food for thought, as well. Remember what I told you about some things better left unknown. If you don't discover what it was that made Velma so desperate to contact you, it could be because the good Lord felt it was for the best."

I hugged her. She felt so small in my arms. "I'll remember. Thank you. I'm so glad you were my gram's dear friend. She was very lucky to have you."

"I was lucky to have known her," she replied. "Would you like me to contact Clayton and have him stop by today to speak with you? I'm sure he'd be honored to have Velma's memorial service at Maple Street Church."

"Yes," I answered. "Please. That would help us out a lot. One less thing to have to handle today."

"We'll be over later on. If there's anything more I can do, let me know."

We hugged again before I went out the door into a crisp October breeze. The scent of autumn reminded me of Grandma Hatcher's homemade doughnuts. How she loved to make a big batch as soon as the leaves turned from green to gold. I crossed her yard and went up the front porch, wishing to find her in the kitchen with her apron on. Most likely she'd scold me for going out without a jacket.

"Annie," Brian said, as soon as I came through the door. "We were just wondering where you were. Suzanne said you probably took a walk."

My attention went to Suzanne, who still looked as haggard as she

23

sounded on the phone last night. We exchanged knowing glances as the boys scampered toward the TV.

"I was at Edna's," I answered, trying to make my voice sound neutral. It was hard to look at my brother, knowing the truth about his marriage. "She made us some tea and we shared some of her fresh baked banana bread. She's such a nice old woman. It makes me wish I'd taken the time to get to know her when I lived here."

Brian widened his eyes. "That would've been a sight. My teenage sister hanging out with a silver-haired old lady. Somehow, that's too much of a stretch."

"I think it would have been nice," Suzanne interjected. "I knew an old woman who was like a grandmother to me where I grew up. She lived a few houses down, but I'd do her ironing twice a week and we'd have these long talks. It was special, actually. I miss her to this day."

"Annie had a grandmother," Brian replied, sounding oddly unsympathetic. "She raised us kids, for goodness sake. Why would she have needed a second grandmother right next door?"

I had the feeling by the frosty glares passing between them that these little squabbles were hardly anything new. Suzanne politely excused herself by saying she was going to see if the boys wanted anything to drink. Brian and I were left alone.

"You look tired," he said, examining my face. "Were you able to get any sleep at all?"

The phone call I made to Suzanne the night before replayed like a recording in my head. He's where he's been for the last six months—living with the woman he loves. Nothing would've told me my brother was capable of such betrayal just by looking at him. He appeared casual and relaxed. The only thing different was the absence of his wedding band, which I was glad he had the decency to remove. If what Suzanne told me was true and he'd taken up a second life with some other woman, wearing his wedding ring around his wife would have been like a stinging slap in the face. It hurt to see the torment that had ravaged their once-loving marriage. I wanted to say something so he'd open up to me, but remembered how Suzanne had asked me not to.

"No. I didn't sleep. There was just too much on my mind."

"Staying here alone doesn't help that," he replied. "I wish you'd stay with us at the house. The guestroom is all made up in case you should change your mind."

We would've played the role of a happy husband and wife, but he would've slept on the floor.

"Thank you, anyway," I said, hoping my discomfort didn't show. "I think I'll be fine here. I need this time to kind of come to terms with my past. So much of it is coming back to haunt me."

"Is it that secret that Grandma Hatcher wrote you about? If it is, maybe you'd be better off to just let it go. She's passed on now and I don't see any way for you to find out what it was. You're just going to drive yourself crazy unless you forget it."

"I think I know what it was," I said, stealing a look at Suzanne serving the boys some more of that orange drink over Brian's shoulder. "I found something last night as I was going through the old family photo album."

His brows drew together as he squinted. "What is it?"

I motioned for him to follow me as I led the way upstairs. His footsteps lagged once we approached the doorway to Grandma Hatcher's room. It was the first time he had been upstairs since she'd died, and I could tell it was very difficult for him.

We stepped into her room and fell silent a moment. I then went to the bookcase and retrieved the photo album, shaking it until the envelope I was searching for slipped out. My breath caught in my throat as I looked back at my brother. It was such a shock when I read it. I could only imagine how he was going to feel.

"Who's it from?" he asked, taking the letter as I handed it to him.

"I think I'll just let you find out for yourself."

Time felt like it came to a slamming halt as he carefully read the writing that came from our mother's own hand. I waited for his reaction for what seemed like forever. He finally raised his eyes to meet mine.

"Why would she keep this from us?" he asked, gulping back tears. "If our mother wanted to ask forgiveness and come back into our lives, why wouldn't Grandma Hatcher have wanted that for us? Do you think she just never wrote her back? When was this letter written?"

I flashed the envelope in front of him, pointing out the postmark. "Twenty years ago. Can you believe it? We were just little then. I was two and you were six, just starting kindergarten. Since our mother never did come back, I guess Grandma Hatcher didn't answer this letter. She kept the truth about our mother from us all this time."

"Do you think this is the secret she was hiding from you? If it is, then why didn't she also want to tell me before she died? It had to do with the both of us."

My thoughts scattered. I hadn't considered that before. What if I was wrong and there was something else? In a way, it was a relief to think I had discovered what it was that had tortured her enough to break down the wall between us and ask me to come home one last time. But, Brian was right. She would've included him in on her confession, wouldn't she? She not only robbed me of my natural mother, but she stole that away from him, too.

"I don't know. Nothing makes sense."

"Have you tried to contact her? We've got the address here. It says she lived on Baker Street in Anaheim, California."

I shook my head. "No. I figured it was twenty years ago and she's more than likely moved on."

"But, it's a place to start," he answered, bubbling with enthusiasm. "Let's try and call long distance information. It's a shot in the dark, but maybe they'll have a listing for a Dorothy Hatcher."

"She could've married somebody and has a different name by now. Maybe she isn't even in California anymore. Besides, I'm not sure what we would say to her if we found her. Have you ever thought of that?"

"Have I ever thought of that?" he echoed, his tone melting to a whisper. "Just a million times a day since I was six years old."

Tears filled my eyes over my brother's raw honesty. "And did you come up with an answer? For what you would say, I mean."

He looked back at the letter he held in his hands. "I'd tell her I love her. That no matter what, I always have. That's the most important thing that I'd want her to know."

"You wouldn't ask why she walked away from us in the first place?"

The answer didn't flow. Instead, it took a moment to emerge. "I know why. She was scared. People do the wrong things when they're feeling so overwhelmed. Must be she didn't think she could give us what we needed, so she had to just up and walk away."

"You act as if you relate to that. How someone can just abandon their loved ones and start a new life." Not telling him that I knew he'd left his family to be with his girlfriend was beginning to feel like I was plugging a leak in a dike with my finger. I was getting weary of holding it back. I wanted to just set all the truths free. Let all of his problems, hurts, and thoughts flood over us so I didn't have to pretend anymore. I longed to help him. Help Suzanne. See their broken dreams pieced back together.

It wasn't my place to interfere, but it was nearly impossible to stay quiet. Too much was going on in our lives that we had no control over, but this was one thing Brian could change. He loved Suzanne with all of his heart. Those boys were his everything. He could stop the foolishness that was tearing them apart . . . swallow his pride and move back home. It was simple to see from where I was coming from. The solution was right in his hands.

"Maybe I can relate," he uttered. "I'm not proud to admit it, but I think I know a little of what she might have been feeling. Sometimes all that responsibility is more than one person can handle."

"You're talking about Suzanne and the boys? The responsibility of being a husband and a father?"

"The responsibility of being everything to everyone. There's nothing left in the end for yourself. Nothing but an emptiness that won't go away."

"Is that why you turned to somebody else, Brian? Is this emptiness inside of you so bad that you'd leave your family and ruin your marriage? I tried to call you late last night when I discovered our mother's letter, and Suzanne had no choice but to tell me you weren't there. She didn't want you to know that she told me about your situation, but I want to help. I think you're all in a lot of pain. Especially the boys. They need their daddy back home, Brian. Not living with some other woman."

The muscles in his jaw flexed as he turned for the door. "I don't want to talk about it. I didn't want to deal with this on top of everything else. If Suzanne told you about our personal business, I'm sorry for that. She had no right. It's the last thing we need to be worrying about when we have a funeral to plan. This mess is between her and I. I'd just like to keep it that way."

To both of our horror, Trevor appeared in the doorway and obviously overheard. His face was flushed and his chin quivered as he tried not to cry. Even at this tender age, he believed a real man didn't show his emotions.

"Mom is making cocoa. It was Josh's idea. She wants to know if you guys want any."

Brian walked over and swiped a stray lock of hair from his son's brow. "We'll be right there. I'm sorry if what your Aunt Annie and I were discussing upset you. I didn't mean for you to hear any of that, you know. It's something only grown-ups have to deal with."

Trevor sadly scowled and broke from his father's touch. "You're wrong, Dad. Josh and me have to deal with it, too. We're the ones who always see Mommy crying because you're not home anymore."

He walked away and left his father behind in a stunned silence. The hurt on Brian's face made me go over and hug him tightly as his arms dangled limply at his side.

"I never meant to hurt anyone," he breathed into my hair. "I was just trying to make the emptiness go away. God forgive me."

"The emptiness won't ever go away if you try and fill it with all the wrong things. You love your wife and your beautiful boys. Running away isn't the answer."

"Nothing makes it go away, to tell you the honest truth," he answered. "I'm all messed up. I wish me, you, and Mom could just start all over. I wish we could be a normal family so maybe I'd know what a normal family really is. Lord knows we never had one growing up with Grandma Hatcher, always wondering why our mother gave us up. I still don't have one now, with my wife and two boys. Why is something so simple, so out of reach?"

"I don't know," I said tearfully, embracing him even tighter. "But, there's plenty of time to work through all of this. We can talk more about it later. Let's go down and get some of that cocoa Suzanne is making. Actually, it sounds pretty good."

He drew back and gave a weak smile. "A shot of scotch would sound even better."

I made a fist and punched him playfully in the arm. It brought back such memories of being kids again, playing, joking, and teasing each other. It was comforting to go back to those times when things were so much simpler. But, Mom still wasn't here when she should've been. She'd never know the wounds her leaving us behind caused. Even if Grandma Hatcher could've reunited us, she never should've left in the first place.

"But, I suppose I'll have to settle for hot chocolate. You can't float marshmallows in a shot glass."

I snapped back from my thoughts and concentrated on my brother's attempt at a joke. "Good point. Then, last one down is a rotten egg!"

Suzanne remained mostly quiet for the rest of the morning. The boys had brought a football and went in the backyard to toss it around while the grown-ups discussed funeral arrangements. Brian was glad to hear that Clayton was going to come by and the service could be held at the church. Something simple and non-formal would be exactly what she wanted. Grandma Hatcher was never one for bells and whistles.

"We also need to go over to the funeral home where the body is," Brian said solemnly. "We need to pick out a casket and after that, contact the florist for the floral arrangements. She loved roses, so I thought that would be nice. Then there's the obituary. We need to call the newspaper so they can run it in tomorrow's edition and also go to Shady Oaks Cemetery and select a plot."

I nodded at the long list he just recited. "Then there's the tombstone, too. We need to choose one and have it engraved."

Brian looked out the window where the boys were in a tackle and then focused back on Suzanne. She sat next to him at the kitchen table, but acted like she wasn't even there. Like she was lost in a place her own husband couldn't follow.

"I kind of think we should've made the boys go to school today," he said to her. "There's so much to do, and—"

"They need to be with us now," she snapped back. "Grandma Hatcher's death has upset them, too. They hardly slept at all last night until I finally had to leave their bedroom light on. There's no way they could have concentrated in school."

"I just don't want to upset them further with all this funeral stuff," Brian responded. "It's not exactly comforting for children to hear about caskets and cemetery plots."

She sat back against her chair and crossed her arms at her chest. "It's nice of you to worry about what will upset them, Brian. I think they can deal with this just fine."

The tension in the air made it difficult to breathe. I took a chug of my lukewarm cocoa and found it almost impossible to swallow. I couldn't blame Suzanne for the icy attitude she had toward my brother, yet it was so hard to witness. They'd always been so loving with one another.

"Of course I worry about them," Brian said firmly. "I worry about them more than you know."

She squirmed a bit as if trying to ward off her anger. "That's touching."

"You know," I intercepted. "If it would make things any easier, I could stay here with the boys while you both go to the funeral home. Edna's grandson is supposed to be coming by, anyway. Someone should be here and I'm sure Josh and Trevor would be happier out in the yard playing football than looking at caskets."

Brian sighed as he thought. "I suppose that makes sense. If you want to go over the plans for the memorial service with Edna's grandson, Suzanne and I can take care of the casket and flowers."

"It'll save time," I answered. "There's so much to do and so many plans to make. This way, we'll get two things done at once."

I saw a polite smile come to Suzanne's lips as she awkwardly looked at me. "Thank you, Annie. It would be better for the twins not to have to go to the funeral home."

"I agree," added Brian. "I think that's a good idea."

"And it will give you two a break," I said, not knowing if I was pushing my limits. "You need time alone without the kids right now. Time to just be together and talk."

"I've been wanting that, too," Suzanne said softly. "Just like we used to do."

Brian paused as if he didn't know how to react, then stood and pushed back his chair. "We'd better get going, then. I'll go tell the boys you're staying here with them while Suzanne and I go into town."

I saw Suzanne dip her gaze to her hands in her lap. "Tell them we won't be long."

Chapter 7

It was less than an hour later when the doorbell rang. I'd just finished making the boys a mid-morning snack and they were busily chatting at the kitchen table. Knowing it was probably Edna and Clayton, I told Josh and Trevor to either stay in the kitchen or go back outside to play since we had important things to discuss.

"Hello, Annie," Edna greeted after I opened the front door. "I'd like you to meet my grandson. Clayton, this is Annie."

He broke into that lopsided grin I saw in the photograph and gently shook my hand.

He was taller than I thought, with dark wavy hair and peaceful eyes just like his grandmother's. I found it hard not to keep staring into them.

"I'm pleased to meet you, Clayton. Edna told me how you were such a big comfort to Grandma Hatcher in her final days. That means a lot, knowing you were here for her."

"She was a special lady," he responded. "Our congregation is going to miss her."

I invited them inside, where we sat in the living room. I offered tea or coffee, but both had already had their fill. That left us to discuss the memorial service, and to my surprise it was very difficult. Instead of planning a tribute to a wonderful woman, I could only see it as saying good-bye.

"I know she loved you very much," Clayton said, noticing my tearful eyes.

I shrugged. "I'm not so sure. I didn't deserve her love, really. I did things that really let her down."

"That's the beauty of unconditional love," he answered. "You can let people down and it doesn't make any difference. Maybe there's disappointment. Maybe there's hurt, but the love is always there."

Edna nodded. "Just like the love you have for her. It's plain to see that has still survived even though you've had your differences."

"It was never a question of love," I said. "I guess it was pride. Stubborn pride. It all seems so ridiculous now."

Clayton studied my expression as if looking for some kind of sign. The weight of his gaze made me slightly uncomfortable.

"I want you to know, Annie, that Velma shared a great deal with me in those days before her passing. She was preparing her soul for the Lord and wanted to confess her sins so she could have the promise of eternal life. She had a great burden that she also wanted to share with

30

you, but unfortunately, she didn't get the chance. She asked me to be the one to tell you in case she did pass away before you got her letter. I told her I would do that."

My chest grew heavy as I struggled to breathe. "I—I've been trying to figure out what could've been so horrible that it pained her so to finally tell me. Her letter was so curious. This secret she had almost seemed to haunt her. She wrote that she would never be able to rest in peace until she shared what she had been keeping from me for all of these years."

"Velma did find peace," Clayton gently assured me. "She knew the wrong she once did was going to be set right. I made her that solemn vow. The last time I saw her before her passing, she had contentment to her eyes that I see all the time with people who are right with their Lord. Believe me, she was set free from the pain that this secret brought her and was ready to go to heaven."

I nervously folded my hands to keep them from shaking. My palms were perspiring as I pressed them together. "Was the secret about my mother? That she wanted to come back to raise my brother and me, but Grandma Hatcher didn't want her to?"

Clayton hesitated. "No. What makes you think that?"

"I found a letter postmarked twenty years ago in the family photo album upstairs. It was written by my mother, saying she had changed and wanted to come home. That she would wait for Grandma Hatcher's answer. If she didn't write back, she'd just figure it was her payback for abandoning us in the first place, but she really wanted to come back. She learned what was important. She sounded like she was ready to love us."

"Velma spoke of that letter," he said, compassion softening his face. "She did respond, Annie. She believed your mother and invited her to come back to have a fresh start with you children, but when she didn't hear from her again, she did her own investigating. She found out your mother had been sent to a California prison to serve time for possession of drugs. That was all she needed to see that her daughter hadn't really changed at all. I think Velma believed that she wanted to, but you and your brother needed security. She dedicated herself to making sure you both had that."

"My mother was in prison?" It was something I didn't want to believe. Of all the images I had of the woman who gave me life, someone caged behind bars was never one of them.

Edna squared my gaze as if she knew I needed to stay focused. "Your grandmother was very hurt when she found that out. She wanted to believe Dorothy had straightened her life out, but once she learned she was serving time in prison, she closed the door to the past and concentrated on you kids. All she wanted was for you both to have a happy life with lots of love. You and Brian were always her first priority."

I couldn't sit still anymore. My muscles were screaming to move, even if it meant pacing slowly and going nowhere. I could hear Josh and Trevor playing in the backyard. They sounded wonderfully oblivious to the seriousness inside.

"Then what is the secret?" I asked, turning to face Clayton. "If it doesn't have to do with my mother, what does it have to do with?"

When he remained silent, fear swam through my veins. He was a pastor. A leader of hurting souls. Knowing the right words during difficult times was supposedly his specialty, yet he looked lost as to what to say. Fearful, almost. For the first time in my entire life, I wondered if having God on one's side was enough. Whatever he had to tell me, why wasn't his faith giving him the strength? How bad could it possibly be?

Edna touched the pearls at her neckline with a nervous hand. "She always wanted to tell you, Annie. She knew what she did was wrong, but she did it solely for your protection. She didn't want you to end up like your mother, with responsibilities you couldn't handle. She wanted you to have a real shot at life."

"I'm lost," I uttered, growing more frightened by the second. "I wish we could just cut to the chase."

Clayton came over and took my hand. His touch was gentle and warm, filled with compassion, but I still felt utterly terrified. I didn't like the dread in his eyes or the rigid way Edna was sitting. They both looked like a bomb was about to drop.

"It's about your baby, Annie," he said carefully, still holding tight to my hand. "The baby Velma told you had died at birth."

My heart stopped as I gaped back at him. What did my stillborn child have to do with this? "I don't understand—what are you trying to tell me?"

"Go back to that night," Clayton continued. "To the moment of your baby's birth. What do you remember about it?"

It was all still so clear. The sound of the rain pelting the window, the smell of the fresh towels Grandma Hatcher had placed under me on the bed, the cool of the moist washcloth that lay draped across my forehead. The pains were so close and unbearably intense. I thought my abdomen was being ripped from the inside and it kept on coming. Harder and harder. Longer and longer. I begged Grandma Hatcher to do something to stop it. I kept screaming that I couldn't take the agony anymore.

"It was a long labor," I recalled, focusing on the floral wallpaper so I didn't have to see Clayton's grim expression. "Very long. It began that morning and went clear into the night. By then, the pain had gotten so bad and I was too tired to push. I was crying. I kept screaming and saying I couldn't take it any more. I wanted Grandma Hatcher to do something to make it go away."

"And what did she do?" he asked.

Flashes of the suffering came rolling back. My stomach would harden with a crippling pain and Grandma Hatcher would shout at me to push. I could feel her hands checking me, seeing how close the baby was to coming, but I couldn't make it. Not one minute more. She finally gave me something for the pain.

"She poured me a glass of water and gave me two tablets," I recalled. "It was a prescription her doctor had given her when she slipped on the ice and broke her ankle the winter before. They were for pain. Very strong. I was happy that she actually still had them."

He nodded and pressed on. "But, they made you groggy, didn't they? So groggy that you actually passed out right after the baby was born?"

"I kept drifting in and out of a blackness," I described. "It wasn't a sleep, exactly. I remember bits and pieces of those final moments. Grandma Hatcher made me hold the bedposts and bear down when she saw the baby's head. It was all so unreal. The pills made me all rubbery. The last thing I remember was her pushing down on my stomach because I didn't have the strength. I believe that was when I finally passed out."

"And when you woke up, what do you remember?"

It was still raining, but my bedroom was filled with daylight. I could hear the sound of the TV coming from downstairs. I was sore. So very sore. I could barely even sit up. The towels were all gone, but there were some bloodstains on my sheets. I wanted to see my baby and called out for Grandma Hatcher, but she didn't come. She didn't answer. I knew I had to go to her.

"It was hard to walk," I described. "I was torn apart. I could tell I was bleeding and I felt very weak. But, all I could picture was my beautiful newborn baby and I had to hold her. I had to get to her, no matter how much it hurt. I thought Grandma Hatcher would be in her chair, watching TV with my precious infant safely cradled in her arms. When I finally made my way down the stairs and saw her sitting there, she wasn't holding anything. Her arms were empty. She just sat in a daze watching one of her soap operas. At first, she didn't even respond when I walked right up beside her. I had to ask more than once where the baby was. It was as if she couldn't hear me at all."

"And that was when she told you that the baby was stillborn?" he asked.

"Yes. I was devastated. I remember feeling faint and falling to my knees. Grandma Hatcher got out of her chair and hugged me tightly against her legs, standing over me and sobbing with all of her heart. I was so sorry that she had called the coroner to come and take the baby. I wished I could've at least seen her. Held her. Touched her little fingers and toes. It was a little girl, just as I knew it was. I always felt I was carrying a daughter. There was no funeral for her because of the shame my pregnancy caused. It was something Grandma Hatcher felt was better left alone. She said she would see to it that my baby was cremated so we could scatter her ashes somewhere pretty in the mountains. So, that's what we did. We drove out to a serene place and said a prayer before I opened the box and emptied the contents. It was so strange. I felt so numb. The wind just carried my precious daughter away."

Clayton led me to the couch when he saw how fragile my grief was making me. Edna dug in her purse for a tissue and smoothed it before handing it to me. The memories were smothering. I tried so hard to leave them all behind, but even in my new life as a career woman in Columbus, even after never going back to Claxton again, I was still that hurting girl who always wondered why her baby had to die. Was it a punishment for my sin with Michael? Was that the kind of God we had? I outraged the heavens by giving away my virginity, so the price for my transgression was the life of my baby?

"You know, I always thought it was my fault." I cried, mopping my tears and trembling badly. "That my baby died because what I did was so dirty. Getting pregnant at fifteen wasn't meant to turn into a happy ending. I knew how much shame my expecting a baby caused Grandma Hatcher.

"I saw it on her face every day. She never said it, but in a way, I think she was relieved my child was stillborn. She was so afraid I'd never be able to handle raising a child so young and on my own."

"She was afraid," Clayton said softly. "Afraid that you would follow in Dorothy's footsteps, overwhelmed by a child you were too young to raise and having it ruin your life. She didn't want that kind of fate for you or for the baby. That's why she saw it as a gift to the both of you to give your baby girl away. Your daughter isn't dead, Annie. She was placed in an orphanage and put up for adoption. She's being raised by a family right here in Claxton. A family that attends our church."

The horror of his words raised something sour in my throat. I felt the need to vomit, yet my body seemed unwilling. Tears washed down my face as I rocked back and forth in place unable to comprehend what I just heard. Grandma Hatcher was a gentle, loving woman. Only a cold-hearted monster would steal another person's baby. She wasn't capable of such a cruel act. Not even close. I remembered the wrenching sound of her crying as we cast the baby's ashes to the wind.

She was as brokenhearted as I was that my child never took her first breath. How could Clayton be telling me that it was all a twisted lie?

"This can't be," I mumbled. "I don't believe you."

Edna came over and put her arms around me. I could no longer tell if her uncontrollable shaking was from the Parkinson's or the nightmare we were talking about. Her hands were icy cold as they grabbed on to mine.

"She prayed on it every day," she assured me. "Velma always suffered so over what she did with the baby. In her heart, it was the right thing to give you all the benefits of freedom that Dorothy never had, but at the same time she knew she had taken God's plan into her own hands. Even when the Thompsons adopted the little baby, it didn't bring her much of a reprieve. It was a secret that always tormented her."

"My baby didn't die?" I echoed, feeling the room around me start to dip and sway.

"She's alive, Annie," Clayton whispered. "I can even tell you her name if you'd like."

I wanted to know. I wanted to hear it. I wanted to repeat it and see how it felt on my lips, but instead all I could do was give in to the dizziness I was feeling and fall into a tunnel of black. . . .

Chapter 8

The first thing I became aware of as my senses staggered back from a sea of unconsciousness were voices all around me. They were foggy at first, far away and garbled, but then they got clearer as I opened my eyes.

"I can't fathom how Grandma Hatcher could do such a thing," Brian said in a tone thick with grief. "She told all of us the same lie. We all believed that baby died at the moment of birth. How could she have deceived us so deeply? How could she have taken Annie's own child away and never said one word to her about it?"

Clayton's words cut in like a boat slicing through choppy waters.

"She did it out of a deep love for Annie. She was a fifteen-year-old child having a child. That was how Dorothy spun so far out of control. Velma ached in her heart about it every day. Her very own daughter got pregnant out of wedlock at a very early age and it drove her to breakdowns and drug addictions. Velma couldn't bear to see that happen to Annie."

I struggled to sit up on the couch and focused on everyone standing near the kitchen. Even the twins were in the group, looking a bit lost and scared.

Suzanne gave them false smiles and fussed with their hair as she listened to the discussion.

It struck me as odd how they were all talking about me as if I didn't exist. My child. My life. The lie that Grandma Hatcher carefully crafted in my defense out of love and protection so I wouldn't turn out like Dorothy.

Anger bubbled inside as I rose to my feet, drawing everyone's gaze my way.

"I want to know her name," I said sternly. "Clayton, please tell me my daughter's name."

For some reason, he looked to his mother before answering.

Her tiny eyes blinked back at him with silent urging to fulfill my request.

Slowly, he walked toward me and then paused.

"Her name is Grace," he answered. "Grace Richards."

My knees began to tremble as I gently sat myself back down.

"Grace," I repeated as gently as a prayer. "It's beautiful. So simple and sweet."

Brian rushed over and sat next to me, pulling me into a strong embrace.

"I'm so sorry, Annie. I had no idea. Grandma Hatcher kept this truth from all of us. I never dreamed your child was alive and living right here in Claxton."

"Grace," I whispered again, just to make sure the moment was real. "I have to see her. Take me to her. I have to see my little girl."

Clayton flinched nervously and grasped for an answer, then walked over and stooped down to level my gaze. In the core of his eyes was a powerful pleading that even my desperate want couldn't ignore.

"It's not that simple, Annie," he said. "Grace sees the Richards as the only mother and father she has ever known. They have given her a wonderful life. I understand how you're hurting and the need you must feel to see her, but you have to put this innocent little girl first. You'd be a stranger that disrupts her world."

A stranger. I bit back my tears as Brian squeezed my hand. Clayton was being honest, but it was hard for me to take. Grace was my own flesh and blood. My very own daughter, yet if she saw me on her doorstep, I'd be nothing but an outsider. She had two loving parents and, according to Clayton, a happy life. Wasn't that more than I could've given her if I had raised her like I had planned? It would be pure selfishness to pop up now and confuse her—even scare her. Threaten the security and happiness that she had.

Yes, I was dying to hold her and breathe in the sweet scent of her. I wanted to soak up everything about her that I had missed in these last seven years. But, to do that, I'd have to get close, and it was far too late for that. Grandma Hatcher stole that gift away from me when she decided to play God with everyone's fate.

"I don't want to hurt her," I answered, letting my tears slide down both cheeks. "That's the last thing I would ever want to do. I just need so much to see her and to know that she's real. All this feels too much like a dream."

"You can," Edna said, making her way into the living room to stand next to her son. "This Sunday, as a matter of fact. The Richards will be in the congregation and Grace will be in Sunday school. They attend faithfully every week."

Clayton nodded.

"They have a strong foundation in Christ and are very active in the church. Mrs. Richards leads our women's group every Tuesday evening and also sews the costumes for our Easter and Christmas shows. Mr. Richards is our youth pastor and the kids just love him. He has a powerful teen program that has grown in the last two years, and the group often volunteers in our community. As much of a shock as you have just gotten about your daughter, I can assure you that she couldn't have been adopted by a more loving and inspirational couple."

"My daughter," I said out loud, half laughing and half crying. My emotions felt tugged at both ends. "I can't believe it. You just don't know how much I've thought of her every day of my life. The day Grandma Hatcher and I gave my baby's ashes to the wind, a part of me disappeared along with them. I just don't know how she could've been so cruel to stand next to me and fake that whole ritual. She knew my baby was alive and well. Her tears were nothing but lies."

Suzanne came forward, her eyes glazed with sadness.

Brian stood up and let her sit in his place. She carefully took my hand inside of hers and gave me a courageous smile.

"As hard as this is to understand, I have to believe in my heart that Grandma Hatcher meant well. She made decisions that weren't hers to make, but her funeral is Friday. We have to remember her with love and compassion, not anger over the lies we've just discovered."

My chin quivered as tears rolled down my face. "It's just so hard now. I want to ask her why, ask her how she could have stood by and watched me mourn the loss of my baby knowing what she did. But she can't tell me. I'll never know. It will be something I'll never come to understand."

"Maybe not," Suzanne replied, blinking through a solemn gaze. "If I were in your place, I know I'd be feeling the same way. But one thing I know for sure, along with everyone else in this room, is that Grandma Hatcher had a heart the size of Texas. When she loved someone, she loved them with every fiber of her being. There was nothing she wouldn't do to protect her family, and I believe that was her only intent. Not to hurt you or rob you of something, but to shield you from the struggle that Dorothy went through.

"It wasn't right and she must have prayed for forgiveness every moment of her life, but she loved you so much, Annie. You were like the daughter she never had. She must have just wanted the moon and stars for you, not a world of burdens. As unbelievable as her choice was, I can only hope you can come to forgive her. If you don't and you hold on to this anger, it will only poison your life."

I stared back at her for several seconds, knowing how well she knew what anger could do to a person. After what Brian had put her and the boys through, she was literally a different woman. She didn't laugh anymore, and her eyes weren't even alive. They seemed like two dull pools of murky water. She was warning me so I wouldn't end up like her and have all joy fade from my life.

I studied Suzanne's expression and then looked over at Brian, who appeared fidgety and uncomfortable. This wasn't supposed to lead back to him and the wrongs he had done to his family, but he knew the wounds his infidelity had created.

Suzanne and the boys were hurt and angry. Brian had let them all

38

down. But what do you do with a heart that's been so badly shattered? Was there ever any mending all the pieces?

"I don't know if I could forgive Grandma Hatcher for what she has done," I said honestly. "How do you do that when it hurts so much?"

Suzanne dropped her gaze to our hands that were still squeezed together. "I don't know, to tell you the truth. I'm trying to find that one out myself."

It was then that Edna caught my attention, and I reflected back to the times she warned me of knowing the truth. She said she knew from experience how secrets could destroy people. I wondered if she possibly held the answer to what to do with a broken heart.

"Did you forgive?" I asked her, catching her off guard. "Someone hurt you deeply. I've sensed it from the beginning. You warned me of knowing the truth, as if you've been in my shoes before. I know it isn't something you find easy to talk about, but I need to know how you made it through and if you did come to forgive. There's a peace in your eyes that I actually envy. I'd like to have that one day."

The room grew silent as Edna slowly sank into Grandma Hatcher's chair. She looked so small and frail compared to Grandma Hatcher's robust build that filled out that chair clear to the arm rests. It was almost disturbing to see someone else sitting there. To my recollection, no one else ever had.

"You see a lot in people, Annie," she said with a weak smile. "Even when they would rather you didn't. You are right when you say that it isn't easy for me to talk about, but I want to help you if I can. I wouldn't be a Christian woman if I didn't at least try."

"Would you rather talk in private?" Brian asked. He acted as if he was eager to leave the room anyway, now that the walls of truth were closing in.

"Perhaps that's best," Edna replied, looking back at the boys, who stood bored by the kitchen doorway. "I think some privacy would be very nice."

Suzanne got up and swiped tears from her eyes. She looked back at me with a wealth of compassion.

"We're going to go now since the boys are getting tired. Brian and I can handle the rest of the calls and arrangements. You have a lot to deal with right now and you need to have time to digest it. Just know that we're here for you if you need us at all. Please call me later if you need someone to talk to."

"Thanks so much, Suzanne," I answered, quite touched by her caring. She was always friendly, but suddenly I felt very close to her. In a way, she was a bigger help to me than my own brother was. She understood how it felt to be a victim of someone else's reckless choices and was there to offer the comfort of understanding.

Brian came up and hugged me, then followed it with a brisk kiss on my cheek. "I hope you'll be okay, Annie. I hate to leave you when you're so upset."

"I'll be fine," I answered with a confidence I wasn't sure I had. "I'm going to talk with Edna for a while and then go over the plans for Friday's service with Clayton. You and Suzanne go ahead and take the boys home."

"If you're sure," he said, smoothing my hair back like Grandma Hatcher used to do. "We'd be happy to stay if you need us."

"I want to go home," Trevor moaned, thinking his father's offer would lead to more boredom. "Can't Aunt Annie call you at Janet's house if she needs you?"

Suzanne's face went white as chalk at the mention of her rival's name.

"Aunt Annie can call us at the house," she swiftly responded. "We'll be there for anything that she needs."

Sadness clouded my heart as I looked at Brian's family so weighted by pain. I wondered how he could continue this situation when the ones he loved were so obviously suffering. Now she had a name, at least. Janet The Homewrecker. I couldn't understand how any decent woman could break apart a good, loving family.

"Yes," I said, awkwardly. "I'll just call over at the house if I need to. But I've got Edna right next door. I'm sure I'll be just fine."

The guilt on Brian's face made it hard for him to look me in the eyes. When he did, I saw a look I hadn't seen since we were kids. That familiar look of abandonment, of fear, of the agony trapped inside every time the topic of our mother came up.

But now the loss he was feeling went deeper than ever before. Now it was his wife and sons who were rapidly slipping away, even if it was by his own doing. Maybe he felt he didn't deserve them, somehow. That since his own mother didn't love him enough to stay, maybe he wasn't worth loving. Something had broken deep inside and was crying out to be fixed.

"I'll see you tomorrow," he whispered as he hugged me good-bye. "I love you."

"I love you, too," I answered back.

The boys waved lazily at me as they followed their mom and dad out the front door. With a long, deep breath I turned back to Edna and Clayton.

"She is right, you know," Clayton said from the sofa, sensing my need for direction. "Suzanne said forgiving is the only way to free yourself of the anger that will poison you. Jesus taught us that lesson as he died on the cross. We need to imagine the suffering and wrong that He endured."

"I'm not a saint, Clayton," I snapped back, unable to control my sudden surge of bitterness. "I can't possibly act so purely. What Grandma Hatcher did was unforgivable. She stole my child away. I'll hate her for the rest of my life."

"There it is," he said softly. "There is the poison."

"Stop!" I cried with frustration as I turned and faced the window.

"It won't stop," he countered. "Not as long as you hold on to the wrong that Velma did. The hate, the poison, the anger, and hurt will be your soul mates forever."

I let a pocket of silence come between us as I tried to gather my thoughts. I felt my emotions spinning out of control. The anger inside of me did burn like an evil flame, but I was entitled to it and refused to let it go.

There was no way I would let Grandma Hatcher off the hook. She didn't deserve to be forgiven. She didn't deserve to be breathing a sigh of relief from the great beyond as I let things go and made her dirty secrets all right.

It wasn't all right. I never got to hold my baby. I thought she was dead for all of these years. I mourned her passing every day of my life. Even though I was only fifteen when I felt my daughter kicking inside of me, I loved her in a way I never felt before.

I would whisper to her at night and sing softly to my rounded belly, hoping she'd hear me. So many times I imagined that first time I would see her, how my heart would overflow.

I knew I'd be the mother I never had. I knew my own child was a part of me that I'd never, ever let go. But I never got the chance to see her or hold her or love her. I never got the chance to be a mother.

If Jesus forgave as he hung on the cross, he probably didn't know the likes of Grandma Hatcher.

"Annie," Edna said, calling my attention back to the chair. She sat shaking, but her gaze was strong and steady. "You asked me whether I forgave whoever hurt me in my past. Would you like me to tell you about it?"

"Yes," I answered, making my way back to the couch. "I would if you're willing."

Edna looked over at Clayton, who stood solemnly as if he knew what she was about to say. Whatever pain Edna had been through, I sensed that Clayton had been through it, too. He walked to the other sofa and sat down before she started. It was almost as if his legs grew unsteady.

"I begged Clayton not to tell you the secrets that Velma had kept from you," she said. "I know how damaging the truth can be and how it can ruin your life.

"I thought it might be best if you just never knew the truth, but

41

he made Velma the promise that he would tell you in case she passed away before you came back home. And my Clayton isn't one to break a promise.

"But, yes, I do speak from experience. An experience that happened long ago, but changed my life forever."

"Did someone hurt you with a secret, too?" I felt my mouth grow dry. So much was happening and it felt like a roller coaster ride with no peaceful end in sight.

She looked down at her hands folded in her lap. They shook uncontrollably as she clasped them together.

"No, not exactly. I was the one who had the secret that hurt someone else beyond repair. It was my daughter. My only child. The woman who was Clayton's mother. She committed suicide because of the truth that I hid from her. I always regretted telling her, since she never had to know. If I kept it to myself, she would have been alive today."

"I don't know if that's true," Clayton interjected. "She was always kind of fragile and suffered with depression as far back as I can remember. When my dad died when I was twelve and it was just me and my mother, she really plunged into emotional problems and often turned to sedatives and alcohol to try and lull them. What she did was her own decision, no matter how much your secret hurt. I never blamed you for what happened to my mother. I just wish somehow, Gram, that you wouldn't, either."

Tears glistened on Edna's powdered cheek.

"And that shows your heart of gold, Clayton. But I can't help but blame myself for her overdose. What I revealed to her pushed her over the edge. I thought it might help her to deal with what happened to her, but instead, the long-buried truth destroyed her."

"What truth?" I asked, wondering if I was digging too deep. "Would you mind sharing with me what kind of secret it was that you kept?"

Clayton watched Edna as she dug in her purse for a tissue. Sympathy softened his expression.

"My mother worked as a bartender in a tavern near where we lived," he said. "She worked there for five years and everyone loved her. But one night as she left the bar in the early hours of the morning, she was pulled behind the bushes by the parking lot and raped by two men. It hurt her bad. She was bloodied and banged up, even spent some time in the hospital while all the newspapers in town carried headlines of her rape. She was so ashamed. Even when the two animals that did it were caught, she still couldn't get past it and recover.

"She pulled away from people and cried most of the time. She never returned to work and stayed home with the drapes drawn. She never smiled, never talked, even shut my dad out completely and never paid much attention to me. I was nine at the time and really needed a mother, but she was like a shell of a person since the rape.

"It was like there was nothing left of her. That's how she stayed for years. Nothing made a difference and our family was really torn apart."

Edna drew a raspy sigh and dabbed at her reddened eyes. "That was when I had enough and decided to get involved. I understood her trauma and how dirty she felt, more than anyone realized. I thought if I told her the secret that I had carried since she was born that it would help her to feel less alone. It would show her that life goes on, but instead it drove her to kill herself. It was simply too much for her to handle."

I got up and went over to the chair where Edna was sitting. My vision blurred with tears as I kneeled down and touched her arm.

"What happened?" I asked.

She looked at Clayton before answering.

"I was raped. That was how I became pregnant with Kimberly, Clayton's mother. It happened when I was in clerical school when I was just a young girl. Abortion was unheard of then, unless you went in a back alley somewhere and wanted to risk bleeding to death.

"My parents allowed me to go through with the pregnancy and helped me every step of the way. We moved, so no one knew anything about us. They made up a story that my husband died overseas in the Army. It took the shame out of it.

"As it turned out, that was the story I told Kimberly, too. Her daddy died before she was born. I just didn't see any reason to tell her the ugly truth about the rape and how she was a product of that attack. It never seemed practical to tell her until she was raped and it caved in her world."

Clayton cleared his throat as if it were clogged with too much emotion.

"She had given up on life. Being raped made her feel unworthy of any joy, any love. All Gram tried to do was tell her the real truth to maybe save her from her pain. By then, it was just too late."

"I thought it would show her that I understood." Edna choked in between muffled sobs. "That I went through what she went through. I knew how it felt to be so violated and suffer from the shame of it all. I finally told her that I conceived her as a result of being raped because I wanted her to know life goes on—you can survive."

"What did she say when you told her?" I asked, drawing closer to Edna and aching at the sight of her tears.

"She took it quietly," she answered, looking at a distant spot on the wall as if reliving the moment. "Almost with no reaction. She did hug me after and thanked me for telling her, but I felt something dark inside. I remember my soul was fearful. It was that night that she swallowed a whole bottle of her sedatives and chased it with a pint of whiskey, leaving Clayton to find his mother dead in the morning."

"My God," I uttered, turning toward Clayton, who hung his head in his hands. "I'm so sorry. That must have been such a horrible thing for you to go through."

He looked up with wetness under each eye.

"I was only fifteen. She was all I had left after Dad died. When I found her that morning, it was like watching my own life end. I felt I had nothing to cling to."

"What did you do?" I asked. "Where did you live?"

He smiled. "I was taken in by my basketball coach and his wife. I was his star player and he believed in me. They opened their home and made me a part of their family. It was then that I went to church for the first time, since they were avid Christians. By my sixteenth birthday, I had been saved and baptized. Through Jesus, I learned to forgive my mother for ending her life and find peace in my heart again."

Edna blinked back with a shine to her eyes. "Clayton lived in Philadelphia with the Robinsons and then went on to Bible College. He knew he wanted to dedicate his life to winning more people over to God. He always wrote to me and let me know how his life was going and we kept in touch. It wasn't until I told him that our church pastor had died suddenly last year that he came to Claxton and became Pastor of the Maple Street Church. Everyone adored him from the very first day. He brought joy back into our congregation. That was about the time Velma started coming regularly. She thought Clayton gave very inspirational sermons and she was drawn to him. They became instant friends."

I walked over to him and sat on the couch to his right.

"And she confided in you about the things she was struggling with? Did she tell you what she had done with my baby?"

"She told me she had sinned. That she carried a great burden and wanted to believe God forgave her. It really wasn't until her illness had progressed and she knew she was dying that she told me what she had done. She was in great pain about it and wanted to tell you the truth, but she wasn't sure if you'd come home or even agree to talk with her at all.

"So she made me promise to tell you about the baby if she passed on without getting the chance. As heartbroken as you are, Annie, as hard as it is to fathom, Velma loved you with all of her heart.

"Maybe too much, it seems, now that we know what she did. She just wanted to protect you from the unhappiness Dorothy went through."

44

"How can you hurt someone like this if you love them so much?" I questioned with anger rippling in my voice. "How can you lie to someone you care about like that?"

"To protect them," Edna replied. "At least you think that you're protecting them until the truth comes out, and then it only hurts them deeper. I lied to my daughter for all those years, making her think her daddy was a war hero who died overseas before she was born. I did it to save her the shame and anger that I knew would plague her for all of her life. As it turned out, it only added to her heartaches. It pushed her over the edge until she killed herself."

"But Grandma Hatcher cried with me as we mourned the death of my baby. She held me after we scattered her ashes in the wind and sobbed with such honesty. To think it was all an act makes me sick. That she knew my little girl was alive somewhere, being adopted into a home of strangers, as I tried to recover from thinking she was stillborn."

Clayton reached for my hand and then cupped it in his. Its warmth immediately comforted me.

"Can you see the big picture here, Annie? So many people have experienced some kind of betrayal or hurt in their lives. Me, you, Gram, my mother, and even your brother and his family seem to be hurting. I don't think any of us get to travel through this life experience unscathed by someone else's mistakes. Some of us crumble under the pain and the depression, like my mother did that night she swallowed the pills. Some of us rise above, finding strength in Jesus and forgiving those that hurt us. We are the ones who find peace. What I pray for is that you will be one of those that rise above and not crumble. In time, God willing, you will come to forgive Velma for the horrible thing that she did. Then, and only then, will you be able to feel free of the past and have your life back again."

Like a wave that couldn't be held back, I gave in to heartfelt sobs. Edna and Clayton handed me tissues and gave comforting words until I finally had no more tears. Tired and numb, I finally sat back and let out a long, calming breath.

"All I want to do is see her," I said softly. "I won't cause her pain or disrupt the loving family she has. I'm so thankful two wonderful parents are raising her, and I know I still couldn't give her that even if I fought to get her back. Just for me, I want to see her and memorize her face in my heart. I'm going to church this Sunday so I can finally see my little girl."

"And what about the funeral service on Friday?" Clayton asked. "Are you going to be able to forgive Velma for what she has done and give her a loving good-bye? If you attend her funeral with bitterness and resentment, it will only tear you apart."

I didn't want to answer. It was somewhat comfortable holding on to the hard feelings since they were so easy. They flowed so naturally and felt so normal. Something soft and forgiving took some digging. I didn't know how or even if I should. It still didn't make much sense. Grandma Hatcher destroyed the only real love I had in my life. She stole away my own beautiful child.

"I can't promise how I'm going to feel come Friday," I carefully answered. "All I can say is I won't let my anger get in the way of the meaning behind her service. She hurt me deeply and took something from my life that I'll never have again. It wasn't her place to do that. At the same time, I don't want to live my life with this horrible anger. I just need time to figure it all out."

"Well, you have a lot to think about," Edna said as she slowly rose up from the chair. "I think Clayton and I should get going so you can have some quiet time. If you need me, please just come right over. My door is always open to you. Just try to remember that we all do things out of love that sometimes turns out all wrong. I did, Annie. Velma did. Probably all of us are guilty of it at one time or another. I'm not saying what she did should be excused. I'm just saying it should be forgiven."

"What's the difference?" I asked as I followed them to the front door.

That was when Clayton touched my shoulder and gave a soft grin. "Maybe you'll learn the difference when you come to church on Sunday," he said. "I just may write my sermon especially for you."

As they went out the door and down the porch steps, I wished tomorrow was Sunday. I'd live my dream then. I'd see my little girl. She would be real and right there in front of me. Smiling through my tears, I closed the front door and hoped the next few days would pass quickly.

"I've waited so long," I whispered in the air. "Grace, beautiful Grace, my precious baby girl."

Chapter 9

Friday brought a cold rain, which suited the atmosphere for a funeral. People got out of their cars at the Maple Street Church donned all in black and huddled under umbrellas. Grandma Hatcher would have liked the gray, gloomy skies weeping on her behalf.

The casket was open and she was displayed in a blue church dress with little brass buttons, but she didn't look like herself. They did something to her hair that wasn't at all like she would wear it, and the makeup was too heavy and in the wrong shade. The only thing that was truly her was the way her hands were gently folded at her waist.

I knew those hands so very well. They had always brushed my tears away, braided my hair, kneaded bread dough, hemmed my dresses, and held storybooks as she read to me each night.

As I stared down at them, I almost expected them to jump from their lifeless pose and reach out for me. I was amazed how much I wished that they would.

"I'm so sorry for your loss," said a tall woman as she lightly touched my arm. "I'm Phyllis Hensley. I was in a prayer group with Velma a while back. She was very special. I recognized you from the photos she showed us. She always told us stories of her Annie. You were the light of her life."

I stepped back from the casket and blinked in surprise. "She talked about me?"

She nodded with a smile. "All the time, actually. She'd be so pleased that you came back to Claxton for her service."

She shuffled on as I looked back at Grandma Hatcher. Even now, she was full of surprises. I had no idea that she would talk so openly to people about me, let alone show a photograph. Wasn't I something shameful that she was better off not mentioning? Didn't I only turn out to be a reminder of her own daughter, getting pregnant in my teens?

Even Suzanne said Grandma Hatcher never mentioned me and often left the room if my name came up. Why would she act so differently with her prayer group?

"Annie," Brian's voice came up behind me. "There's someone here who wants very much to meet you. I think you might feel a whole lot better if you did."

A young woman stood off to his side, her hair swept up with thin strands grazing her temples and looking rather thin in a simple black dress.

She looked at me intently with eyes so bright that I assumed she wore contacts. I outstretched my hand to her, hoping Brian would at least give me her name. It was awkward not knowing who she was.

"Hello, Annie," she said. "I'm so pleased to finally meet you."

I shook her hand and still waited for her name. "Do I know you?"

"No, but I know you. You gave me the most beautiful gift of my life. I'm Mrs. Richards. I'm Grace's adoptive mother."

My stomach flinched as if an imaginary fist had just plunged into it. I quickly drew my hand back and fought the urge to run. I wasn't prepared for this. Not today.

Sunday was going to be the day to face this, when I attended church to see my daughter and meet the people who had given her a home. It didn't occur to me that they might be at the funeral. Perhaps my mind was getting too clouded.

I gaped at my little girl's mother and searched for words to say.

"I—I didn't know you knew who I was. Usually information on the birth mother is kept secret."

Her smile was genuine and put me at ease. "Velma told me about you just before her death. I came to see her when she was bedridden in her home. We prayed a great deal together. That was when she told me that she knew the little girl my husband and I adopted was your daughter. She showed me your picture and I knew right away it was true. She looks just like you—especially in the eyes. I hope this isn't too hard for you."

Something melted like April snow in the depths of my hurting soul. My baby looks like me? We have the same eyes? My throat convulsed with unshed tears as so many words wanted to come out. So many questions about the child I'd never seen. I hugged my arms tightly around myself to keep my nerves in check.

"I won't lie to you, Mrs. Richards," I answered. "It's very hard, indeed. There hasn't been a moment in these last seven years that I haven't thought of her. That I haven't missed her. I had no idea that she was even alive. This is just so much to try and take in."

"Velma told me what she had done," she replied with sympathy in her tone. "She cried as she confessed, and I cried along with her. All this time, as we raised Grace, we thought God had just placed her in our hands, but once I learned of Velma's wrongdoings, I started to feel guilty. Like I took something from you—without realizing it, of course. But I still shared a life with the child that you never got the chance to know."

Tears rivered down my face as I looked around the church.

"Is she here? I've wanted to see her. I promise that I won't let her know who I am or upset her in any way."

"No, she isn't. She stayed at home with my husband. We felt she was too young to understand a funeral service."

I admired the protective way her eyes gleamed as she explained that to me. It was clear that she loved Grace with all of her heart. Already, that was something that we had in common.

"I'm glad," I said. "This would be upsetting to a small child."

"Especially a child like Grace," Mrs. Richards said with a slight chuckle. "She is a timid little thing, almost afraid of her own shadow. This would certainly frighten her. She is so sensitive to things that she doesn't understand. Even sitting on Santa's lap still makes her cry."

I could have soaked up everything she told me about my daughter. It made me smile because I was a timid child, too. Grandma Hatcher had to finally push me down the slide at the playground because I was always too afraid to do it.

"She must be in school," I said, needing to know so much. "How does she like it? Does she get good grades? Does she have a nice teacher?"

"Her favorite subject is art. She is very quiet and creative. My husband and I joke that one day she'll be a famous artist with her paintings for sale in Paris. Her first grade teacher's name is Miss Walden, and Grace simply adores her."

Mrs. Richards paused and then let her eyes pool with worry. She seemed to hesitate on her next question as if she were afraid of the answer.

"Where do things go from here? This is an awkward situation, but my heart goes out to you. This must be so hard to handle. I just don't know what to expect now that the truth is out."

"I'm not going to fight for custody, if that's what you're asking," I answered. "As much as I wish I could raise her and be her mother, I truly believe what she has with you and your husband is far better than what I could offer her. She deserves two parents, a secure and loving home. You're her mommy and daddy. The only ones she has ever known. I could never rip apart the family you've become. As much as it breaks my heart to stay a stranger in her life, it's best for her. She's happy now. That's most important."

Mrs. Richards swiped tears from her face and drew in a long breath. "She's our world."

I choked back my emotions. "And you are hers."

"We'll talk some more," Mrs. Richards said softly, hugging me close. "I want you to be a part of her life, too. We'll just take it one step at a time."

Clayton walked up and hugged Mrs. Richards before turning and doing the same to me.

"I'm glad you both have met. I'm sure you have so much to talk about."

"She's wonderful," I said, staring back at my daughter's mother.

49

"It comforts me to see how loved Grace is."

"And now she has even more love than before," Mrs. Richards answered, her chin quivering as she stifled her tears. "I believe God brought you back into her life for a very special reason. We just need to see where all the puzzle pieces fit."

The pews had filled and the organ music had faded.

Clayton glanced at the clock. "It's time to start the service. Velma would have been pleased to see such a fine turnout. She had a lot of people who loved her." He stared directly at me before he turned and walked away.

I took a seat in the first row where Brian, Suzanne, the twins, and Edna all sat closely together.

My gaze kept drifting to the mahogany casket as if so many answers rested in there. The whys, the hows all jumbled together and formed a knot in my gut. Grandma Hatcher looked so peaceful. In a way, it was unfair. I felt as if she went on to heaven and left me floundering in hell.

The words Clayton wrote to honor Grandma Hatcher were lovely. He described her strong spirit, her giving heart, her warm and comforting nature. He even drew a quiet round of laughter when he mentioned her stubborn streak, too.

There were several of her favorite hymns sang by the choir, and Clayton closed with a prayer. He then welcomed anyone to come forward and share any stories or sentiments.

Many of Grandma Hatcher's church friends spoke of their experiences, and Brian and Suzanne even shared some personal family stories.

I knew it was expected of me to go up and say something, but I just couldn't. I was too confused. How could I speak of her love and kindness after what she did?

I decided to stay in my seat and keep my focus to the floor. It was then that I heard a woman's voice.

"I have something to say," she stated.

A figure in black with a black kerchief over her hair walked down the center of the aisle. Everything grew silent as she took the podium and gazed at the open coffin. She was somber and mysterious. I didn't notice her in the church before. Something about her felt almost familiar. I felt myself trying to swallow nervously as I waited for her to speak.

"Who is she?" I heard Edna ask Brian in a whisper.

He hunched his shoulders to show he didn't know. His eyes were as riveted on the woman as mine were. I wondered if he felt something familiar about her, too. She looked out at the mourners in the pews and then slowly slid off her kerchief. Her hair was short, her face full, and her frame slightly hefty. Her eyes darted about the room and then settled directly on me. When they did, I squirmed a bit as I sat, uneasy with the sudden attention.

"I have something I'd like to say about this special woman we are honoring today," she said boldly. "I'd like to say the four words that never came before now. Simple words that most of you say every day, but have always come so hard for me."

I leaned over toward Brian. "Have you ever seen this woman before? How did she know Grandma Hatcher?"

"I don't know. I don't recognize her," he answered.

Edna looked at us both with a curious expression. "Who on earth is she?"

The woman at the podium kept her gaze on our pew, watching us speak softly amongst ourselves.

"Four words," she repeated, again staring right at me. "I'm so sorry that they come so late. I just pray she can hear me from wherever she is. Mom, I love you."

"No!" Brian gasped, reaching out for my arm.

I was numb and barely felt it.

"It can't be. Lord, no. It can't be her."

I began to tremble and leaned against him.

"She's our mother," I uttered, staring at her through my tears. "That woman is our mother."

Silently, she stepped down from the altar and made her way to the casket, leaning over to kiss Grandma Hatcher's cheek.

She then came over to where Brian and I were sitting and gave a gentle smile.

"Four words," she said gazing at the both of us. "I never said them to my own children, either. I love you, Brian. I love you, Annie. I always have, no matter what you believe."

And then, just as suddenly as she appeared, she left. The double doors to the church closed behind her. I wanted to run after her, throw myself into her arms, but all I could do was sit in a state of shock as Brian began to softly cry.

Edna leaned forward, peering at my brother and I. She reached out and touched both of our hands.

"Now we just have to get you both to say three words right back to her. For your own sake, you need to say, 'I forgive you.'"

Brian and I left our seats and hurried outside the church doors to find our mother waiting on the concrete steps. She must've known we'd come. Despite the years that we'd been separated, we were still connected.

The first thing that struck me was how much Brian resembled her, right down to the shape of the eyes. I had her nose and the shape of our mouths were similar, but the one thing we all shared in common the most was a loss of what to say.

She moved toward us timidly. "You're both as beautiful as I imagined you would be. I was so very anxious to see you."

"I can't believe you're here," I blurted as my eyes filled with tears. "How did you know Grandma Hatcher passed away?"

Her smile was gentle and weighted with sadness. "I wrote to her several weeks ago for the first time in a long time. I wasn't even sure if she would open it and read it, let alone respond. But I got a letter back from her telling me how ill she was and that she wanted me to come back to Claxton. To my amazement, she went on to tell me how much she loved me. She said she forgave me for my wrongs and didn't want to go to her grave without telling me so. She even included photos of the two of you."

Brian glanced at me. "We knew you wrote to her a long time ago when we were little and wanted to come back. Annie found the letter in one of Grandma Hatcher's photo albums."

Immediately, she nodded. "I was constantly writing letters to her with promises I couldn't keep. They all ended up in the trash, except that one. I thought if I mailed it, it would somehow make everything I said inside of it true. I'd be the kind of mother you both deserved and never follow the wrong path again. Shortly after that letter was mailed, I was arrested and sent to prison. As much as I wanted to be the parent that the both of you deserved, my spirit was simply too weak."

Brian shifted his stance and his posture grew rigid. "Well, we did okay. Grandma Hatcher gave us everything we needed. She loved us and gave us a home."

"But you didn't have your mother," she answered, blinking back tears of regret. "As good as she was to you, that was always the one thing missing. I don't expect you to understand what made me do the things I did. I don't expect you to even want to hear my reasons. I just want to tell you both that not one day went by that I didn't think of you and wonder how you were. The two of you were always in my heart."

I didn't know how to feel once she said that. The words were genuine and something I always dreamed of hearing from her, but now that they were real and we were standing face-to-face, the moment felt oddly surreal. My emotions went numb. I couldn't find any words to respond with. All I could do was look at Brian and see that he had no real response, either.

"I'm staying in Claxton indefinitely," our mother added. "I'm at the Mountain Lodge in room 112, in case either of you want to reach me. I know how sudden this is and that you weren't prepared to see me. I just hope once you have time to think about it, you'll want to talk some more. We have so very much to catch up on."

"Aren't you going to the burial?" I asked.

She shook her head and glanced out at the trees bowing in the breeze. Only a fine drizzle continued to fall. "I told her what I came to say. It will probably be best if I just go back to my motel."

"But I want you to meet Suzanne and the boys," Brian said. "I don't want you to leave before they have a chance to see you."

"That's just it," she replied. "I'm not going anywhere. I'm staying right here until you or Annie tell me you want me to leave. Otherwise, I'm never leaving either one of you again. I'd like to show you the person that I've finally become. The Mountain Lodge. Room 112. I'll be waiting."

She hugged us both and hurried off. Brian and I stood silently as we watched her flip up the collar of her coat and dip her chin, darting through the maze of parked cars in the lot before finally coming to one and unlocking the driver's side door. She slid behind the wheel and cranked the engine, waving to us as she drove off.

"Wow," Brian muttered, still looking in the direction of her taillights. "I can't believe she's back. She's here."

"Do you believe her?" I asked, almost ashamed at my lack of trust. "Do you really think she's here to stay and would never disappear on us again?"

"I do," he answered firmly. "And do you want to know why?"

"Considering that she's never been able to change before, I guess I'd really like to know your reasoning."

"Because she was able to walk into this church, face everyone, and tell her mother that she loved her. She finally said the words. She never would've been able to do something like that before. And she came right up to us and told us that she loved us. It couldn't have been easy after all of these years, but she did it. That shows courage and that shows change. Most of all, that shows what is in her heart. No matter how leery we may feel, I do think we ought to give her a chance. She's our mother, Annie. Maybe she hasn't been the greatest, but she's still our mother. I say we should at least go to the motel and spend time with her."

"Time," I echoed, almost whispering the word to myself. "The one thing that's so impossible to get back once you waste it. Our mother lost all those years with us. I threw away the last four years of my relationship with Grandma Hatcher, and because of her unthinkable secret, I've missed every year of my own daughter's life. Time is as precious as the air that we breathe, yet it gets thrown away so easily."

Lowering his head and staring down at the pavement between his shoes, Brian nodded. "That's true. I'm guilty of wasting it myself. Time with my boys and with my wife."

"You don't know how lucky you are, Brian," I said to him, sadness aching a knot in my throat. "You have your children right there. You have a family. I'd give anything to be able to hug my daughter, watch her grow, and hear her call me mommy. I'd give anything to have a marriage and build a future with someone. What you and Suzanne have is very special and can set a fine example. Your boys need the very thing you and I never had. A real mother and father."

His jaw flexed as he kept his gaze to the ground. "I've made a mess of things. I don't even know if they want me to come home. I don't know if it's too late after all I've done."

"They love you," I assured him. "That's why they hurt so much. As long as there's love left, it's never too late."

He looked up at me with such need simmering in his eyes. "I hope that's true, Annie. Because if it is, all of our family's wounds can be healed just as simply. You could forgive Grandma Hatcher, we could both trust and forgive our mother, and the past could be left behind. Is it that easy? Just to love and forgive? Will you be able to do it?"

Chapter 10

He went back inside the church, leaving me alone with his questions. They chilled me more than the gray rain. How could I make him believe that his own wife and sons would forgive and accept him back when I couldn't forgive Grandma Hatcher? How could he believe in new beginnings if I didn't believe our own mother could change? My mind swirled in dizzying circles as I drew a deep breath.

"Annie?" Clayton said, stepping outside with a worried expression. "Are you okay? I was concerned when you didn't come back inside. Seeing your mother must've been quite a shock."

There was something about just being near this man that comforted me. The pain I tried so hard to conceal suddenly broke free as I folded into his arms. "Why does everything have to be so hard? Why is my family such a mess?"

His hand went up and softly stroked my hair. "It's not the trials that matter, Annie. Don't you see that? It's where we allow them to lead us. The bad things that happen may not be in our control, but it is up to us what we do as a result of them. Do we let the hurt turn us into bitter people with vengeance in our hearts, or do we learn and grow and forgive as Jesus taught us? You're much too beautiful to let anger and hatred consume you. I wouldn't want you to be bound in the past."

I pulled back and looked into his eyes. "You think I'm beautiful?"

A nervous smile spread on his lips before sliding lopsided as it always did. His sudden embarrassment was equally adorable. "That part wasn't supposed to sneak out. Up until now, it was my little secret."

"I'm glad you told me," I answered, something funny tickling my heart like a fist full of feathers. "Secrets aren't good for people, anyway. They only make life more complicated."

"I do feel better," he said, gazing at me intently. "After all, I always preach how the truth shall set you free."

Awkwardly, I drew back and fussed with my necklace to busy myself. The chill I felt only moments before was now a blazing inferno.

"I don't know why I made such an issue of it. I mean, whether you think I'm beautiful or not isn't of any importance. To be blunt, it's not like there would be any sense in considering something happening between us when I live in Ohio and you're here in Tennessee and I have all this stuff to straighten out in my life. Then again, I'm reacting like you just proposed marriage when all you did was say that you liked the way I look. I guess I'm not used to getting compliments from a man. I'm really botching this up, aren't I?"

His laughter was wonderful. It put my nerves at ease. "I find you very refreshing, Annie. Believe me, women usually aren't as open with their thoughts and feelings when they speak with me. They can't separate the pastor from the man, I guess. Just because I've dedicated my life to the work of the Lord doesn't mean I don't crave someone special to talk with and share with. It doesn't mean that I don't wish I could fall in love."

Even the notion of love used to make my heart shut down. After what happened between Michael and myself, I was convinced that being in love with someone meant paying a dear price. It had to hurt. It had to end badly. Nothing would ever stay the same. To my surprise, as I gazed back into Clayton's eyes, a calm flowed through me as if it were coming from someplace else. Almost like fate taking control.

He won't hurt you, Annie, my mind told me. This time it's right. Trust him. . . . Let go of your fears, and trust and accept the gifts that he's giving you.

"Oh, my," I gasped, stunned by the voice my soul could hear so clearly. It scared me how subtle, yet powerful, it was.

Clayton cocked his head and squinted in confusion. "Is something wrong?"

"No," I answered as my heart raced at double time. "I'm just jumpy, I think. So much has happened lately. I just need time to sort it all out."

"Seeing your mother must've been difficult. I hope you had a chance to talk with her and maybe begin the healing process."

"Yes." I nodded. "Brian and I caught her before she left and we're going to meet up with her at her motel later today. I'm not sure if we should believe anything she has to say. I mean, she wrote to Grandma Hatcher all those years ago promising she had changed when she really hadn't. I don't want to get our hopes up only to be let down. Brian and I couldn't handle that."

"You won't be let down. Her words are genuine. The changes she has made are real this time."

"How do you know?" I asked, envying how sure he seemed.

His face softened and took on that contented look that people with a faith in God always seemed to have. "God spoke to me last night as I prayed about this service today. He told me that your mother would come back, and that this reunion would pave the way for a new beginning between Brian, Dorothy, and you. When God tells me things and I know it's of His doing, there's no doubt it can be trusted."

I reflected back to the startling whisper I heard in my soul about Clayton not hurting me and that I could trust in this attraction. That this relationship was going to be the right one. Was that what it was like to hear God speak directly to you? Was that the voice I was hearing?

"When God speaks to you," I said slowly, almost afraid to ask such a personal question. "What does it sound like?"

"It's not a sound," Clayton answered. "It's more of a feeling in my heart and soul."

"A feeling that something is right and that you can trust it. A feeling so strong that you know you can't deny it. A peaceful whisper, so to speak, right?"

That crooked smile caught me off guard again. "Right. You just know when it comes from God."

The door behind Clayton popped open and Brian stuck his head out. "The choir is finishing up their final hymn and the pallbearers are going to be taking their places."

"I'm coming," I said, almost hating to break the connection I felt so strongly between Clayton and I. "Just give me one minute."

The organ music faded as the door slipped shut again, leaving Clayton and I once again alone. I was never the type to be forward or suggest a date, but this moment wasn't ordinary. It wasn't in my control. It had to have been God playing matchmaker. I swallowed nervously and met his steady gaze.

"I'd really like it if we could get together and talk some more," I said. "It's nice getting to know you—not just the pastor, but the man."

His hand reached out and squeezed mine with a warmth that spread through my veins like honey. "Would you mind if I came by the house tonight? Maybe we could share a cup of coffee with our conversation."

"Tea," I corrected. "That's all Grandma Hatcher has in her kitchen. Of course, if you would rather have coffee, I could pick some up later today. Anything you'd like would be no problem."

"Actually, I'd like some of Velma's tea. I shared many a cup with her during the visits I made in her final weeks and grew rather fond of it."

"Then I'll have the kettle on. Say, seven tonight?"

"I'm looking forward to it," Clayton answered.

"Me, too." My face felt flushed. Not only was it amazing to be feeling an attraction of any kind, especially during my own grandmother's funeral, but to a pastor?

Trust me, Annie, this one is right—you and Clayton will achieve great things together.

I nodded back to that whisper inside me that Clayton couldn't hear. I wasn't about to argue with the voice of God.

Chapter 11

Brian and I arrived at the Mountain Lodge shortly after three and knocked on the door of room 112. Our mother promptly opened it and broke into a wide smile. She was now far more casual in jeans and a white pullover sweater. The TV was blaring a game show in the background.

"I'm so glad you both came," she said, standing back and ushering us inside. "Please, come in. I got some sodas from the machine and stuck them in a bucket of ice, just in case. I didn't know what you liked. I hope cola is okay."

Just that simple comment picked at the wounds. She didn't know what we liked. She didn't know us at all. Her own children and she had no clue about anything in our lives.

I grew uneasy about being there and already wished that we could leave, until I remembered what Clayton had told me about this reunion paving the way to a new beginning. It was just going to be a bit rocky getting there.

"I know it's been a trying day with the funeral and all," she said sympathetically.

Brian shrugged. "It went well. She would've liked the service, and her plot in the cemetery is under a big, old oak tree. She's at peace, which is a comfort."

I found myself tensing up even more. Grandma Hatcher was at peace, but her secret stole my child away and left me hurting like I've never hurt before. Where was my peace now? The torment of my emotions seemed never ending. It was as if she dropped a bomb in my lap and my life blew to pieces, just as she slid off peacefully to heaven.

"Annie?" my mother said, reaching out to softly touch my arm. "Are you all right? You look a million miles away."

Tears burned my eyes as I blinked back at her. "No, I'm okay. I'm just very emotional with all that's going on. Grandma Hatcher's passing and now seeing you after all of these years. It's just a lot to take in."

She looked at Brian and me with so much pain and regret. There was a wall of awkwardness between us, but she seemed determined to scale it.

"You know," she said, taking both of our hands. "I want to be a part of your lives even though I've missed out on so much. I realize you have bitter feelings and a lot of hurt over my leaving you so young, but I wasn't ready. I didn't know how to take care of myself, not to mention two innocent children. I had a drug addiction that consumed my life. I used and I used until I didn't know who I was or what I was doing. I had to hit rock bottom and go to prison for several years to realize how out of control I had gotten.

"If there's any place that makes you come face-to-face with yourself, it's a six-foot by nine-foot prison cell. For once in my life, there was no place to run. No place to escape reality. There were no drugs and no alcohol. No crutches to lean on. All I had was a Bible and myself. The miracle of it all was that I had to go to prison to find the very high I've always craved. It was in God all along. The one thing to fill my emptiness."

I wasn't prepared to have her bear her soul to us in the first ten minutes of our visit. We were virtual strangers. I counted on some kind of chitchat, but not a raw discussion of our mother's deepest feelings and lessons she had learned from living a life of hell.

My chin quivered as I looked back at her.

"Don't all prisoners claim to find God only to go back to their old ways once they're out in society again?" I asked.

She smiled and led us over to the edge of the queen-sized bed where we could all sit and then she switched off the TV. I saw that Brian was growing more and more emotional, twitching his jaw muscles and fighting back tears. It looked like he was going to crack.

"Your observation is probably on target for some," our mother answered. "But while I was living between those dreary cement walls, I saw a great many wonderful transformations. Women who have done horrible things in life like kidnapping, robbery, murder, or running drug rings all had one thing in common before their sentencing. They were lost. Like me. Always looking for that certain something to make them feel good and ending up in all the wrong places.

"Once they started serving their time and everything was stripped from their lives, a learning process took place that never could have in the outside world. A process of loss and isolation. Of seeing who you really are and finding that the only place to turn is in the direction of God.

"Hearts are truly changed when you sink as low as a human being can go. When you're nothing but a number in a prison jumpsuit behind bars, there is no lower place you can fall. It changed me and it changed a great many of the women I bonded with in there. The sad thing is that it takes going to prison for so many to find what they're looking for."

Brian nodded as tears flowed down his cheeks. "I can relate to that lost feeling. I've been lost my whole life. I didn't end up doing drugs or anything like that, but I understand trying to fill an emptiness inside with all the wrong things. It just makes that void in my soul deeper."

Now I was stunned. Brian had been so closed up about his personal problems since I had come to Claxton. Yet, in just a few minutes with our mother in a small motel room, he was sharing some of the pain he'd been feeling. It angered me for a moment, to the point where I almost said something, but then decided not to. There was a reason why he felt safe enough to share with the woman we hadn't seen in so many years. A reason I longed to understand.

Our mother swiped a tear of her own as she gazed lovingly at the two of us. "I want to know my children. I want to know what I've done to you. What hurts you have. How has my walking out on you when you were so small affected your lives? That's where I want to begin, by having time together today. I want you to open your hearts and let me inside, even if they're broken and fearful."

Suddenly, Brian stood and raked a hand through his hair. His breathing was labored and I thought I saw him shaking. His walls of resistance were tumbling down.

"I'll tell you flat-out how it affected my life," he answered, unwilling to look at the woman he was unloading on. "It always made me feel unworthy. Unlovable. If my own mother didn't love me enough to keep me, then who else would? Sure, I found a special woman when I met Suzanne in school, and we had a solid relationship. We married and had children, but deep inside I felt something lacking. I was restless. I couldn't accept that her love was real. I didn't trust it or believe it because I didn't feel like I deserved it."

"Why couldn't you just explain that to Suzanne?" I asked him. "She would've understood that and even gone with you to get help. All you had to do was reach out."

Our mother shook her head. "It's harder to do than you realize. I truly believe that real change happens after a person hits bottom and loses the things that mean the most to them. Is that what happened to you, Brian? Did you self-destruct and lose the things you loved?"

His sobs came in jagged puffs. I'd never seen him so vulnerable and honest with the demons inside him. "Yes," he choked. "I validated feeling so unlovable by finding women who were willing to love me. Most were for one night, some for a longer fling.

"Now I've been living with one because it got so out of control. I liked the attention she always gave me and how I felt when I was with her, and she refused to have a sordid affair. She wanted the real home thing, and for me to prove I wasn't just using her by leaving my family and living with her, so I did. I don't know why. It was stupid, and I hurt my wife and boys.

"Now my family is torn apart and I don't see any way to come back. And the funny thing is that I still feel unlovable and empty. Having a mistress and sex and attention doesn't take it away."

"It did for a little while, right, Brian?" my mother asked, walking over to him to square his gaze. "Like a high from cocaine or a buzz from a bottle of gin. It soothes that empty spot for a little while until it wears off and leaves you crashing with a thud back in the reality you were trying so hard to run from. Other women were your drugs. Infidelity was your high, but the effects have worn off and now you're back where you started, except with a bigger mess of a shattered marriage and family. You keep digging that hole a little bit deeper. I understand that only too well."

"And it's all because of you," he shouted, crying in between his words. "Why didn't you love me enough to want me? Why did you leave me and Annie like a sack of dirty laundry on Grandma Hatcher's doorstep and never once come back to get us?"

I clenched my hands together in my lap, hating the jagged resentment I heard in my brother's voice because I felt so much of it myself. Resentment toward my mother and resentment toward Grandma Hatcher. Both had ruined my life.

"I left my own children for the same reason you left your children, Brian. Because I was looking for peace in all the wrong places."

"I didn't walk out on my children," he shot back. "I've been in their lives even though I moved out. I've still been a father to them."

"Have you?" our mother questioned. "I don't know how that could be possible if you are parking your shoes under another woman's bed. Yes, you probably visit them regularly and are just a phone call away, which is far more than I left you and Annie with, but do these boys feel like they have a real father? Are you there during the night when they have a bad dream? Is your toothbrush next to theirs in the holder?"

"That's not what matters," he said back. The tone of his voice was growing weak and uncertain, as if he didn't believe the truth of his own statement.

"Isn't it?" Our mother went back and sat next to me on the bed. She kept her eyes focused on Brian. "Those things may seem trivial, but those are the things that give a child security. Knowing a parent isn't merely a slot of time for a visitation, but always there to lean on twenty-four hours a day."

Anger welled inside of me like a bomb aching to detonate. She had no right to speak to Brian about good parenting when she was such a failure herself.

"That's not fair," I snapped. "You certainly aren't an authority on parenthood. What makes you think you can judge Brian after the horrible things you've done?"

The room fell quiet. We could hear the hum of the maid's vacuum on the floor up above us and the sound of moving furniture. It was the lull in the storm of too many tender emotions. It was just too soon to be dealing so personally with each other.

"We'd better leave," I said to Brian. He already moved toward the door.

"I didn't mean to chase you away," our mother said, rising to follow us. "I never meant to come on so hard and heavy. This will take time, I know. We have a lot of things to deal with. I just have to remind myself that it won't all be resolved in one day."

Brian paused and turned toward her with his jaw firmly set. "It may not even happen in a lifetime."

"I think it will," she responded with a knowing smile. "It won't be easy, but I have no doubt that it will."

Chapter 12

W e went to the car and got inside as our mother watched from her doorway. I cranked the ignition and jolted the car in reverse, eager to get away and not have the weight of her stare on my shoulders. I needed some air to breathe. Some time to let my rattled nerves settle. I needed to stop thinking of the things that she said.

"That went well," Brian said sarcastically. "Here I thought I was the one who really forgave her and I'd be so happy just to pick up where we left off if she ever came back, and I end up lashing out at her with all this pent-up anger. That was the last thing I expected to do."

I glanced at him before returning my gaze to the traffic ahead. "Maybe it was the last thing you expected, but it must've been the first thing you needed. Were we really all supposed to sit and be civil when she abandoned us and wrecked our lives? Come on, Brian. That's just not possible. She asked us to tell her how her absence from our lives hurt us and made us feel. At least you had the guts to tell her. I didn't. I just sat there like a coward."

"The things she told us," he said, looking out his window at the storefronts whizzing by. "It's hard to imagine what she went through. Being in prison and having nothing. I don't know about this God stuff, though. She makes the answer to life's problems awfully simple. If everyone could fill their empty place by merely opening a Bible and reading the pages, then why doesn't everyone do it?"

"I don't know," I answered, lost in my own spiral of questions. "Maybe because they are still left with choices."

"Choices? I don't follow."

"Choices," I repeated. "Things to choose from to fill that spot. For those outside in the free world, we have a smorgasbord of things to ease our hurts and dull our senses. You chose other women. Our mother chose drugs. I chose falling in love with the wrong man simply because he was the first one who said he loved me. It felt so real that I let myself get pregnant because I was trying to fill a void. But in prison, there is no smorgasbord laid out before you. No booze, no drugs, no parade of sexual partners. Just a cold, dismal cell and you. There's nothing to reach for anymore except the Bible. It's the only life raft they toss you in there."

"Do you believe that's the answer?" Brian asked. "Does God really fill the emptiness?"

I reflected back to that tranquil look I admired in Edna's eyes. The calm in Clayton's voice, the warmth from the people in the church, and even the peace I could sense in our mother. It was something that glowed like a lighthouse in the fog, guiding other lost souls to safety.

"I think I'm beginning to want to learn," I answered carefully. "I've always sensed something different in people who have God as their foundation. It's as though they have a sparkle to their eyes, a calm to their soul, no matter what they're dealing with. I envy that and need it more than ever in my own life. Nothing else seems to be the answer."

Without words, Brian reached over and cupped my hand in his. Maybe he didn't say it, but I could feel how much he needed it, too. Our prison wasn't cement walls like our mother had, but we were both trapped in unhappy lives and longed for a way out.

By the time we pulled into Grandma Hatcher's driveway, Brian and I both had done a lot of thinking. The session at the motel may not have gone very smoothly, but it did open a door that we needed very much to trudge through. A door of truth and self-exploration. No more denial like we had clung to for so long.

"Would you like to stay for dinner?" I asked as we strolled to the front door. "I've got some canned stew inside and could whip up some biscuits. I'm sure Suzanne doesn't feel like cooking after such a long and emotional day."

He stopped and stared at the house in a funny way. "No," he said with a faraway look to his eyes. "If you don't mind, I think I'll take my wife and boys out for dinner. Our lives are in a shambles and I know I have no right to expect they would want to go to dinner with me, but something tells me to do it. Something says to take the chance."

I grinned. "Is that certain something that tells you to take the chance like a knowing whisper to your soul? Like something you can't deny and like some outside source making the decision for you?"

"Exactly," he responded, his brows riddled with curiosity. "How did you know that?"

I placed an arm around him and began walking us toward the front steps where Suzanne and the boys appeared at the door. "Because I'm beginning to understand what that is and what it means. I'll explain it to you sometime."

"Mom's going to order a pizza for all of us," Trevor called out. "Aunt Annie, do you like pepperoni on yours?"

Brian turned to me with second thoughts. "Maybe my idea wasn't the best one. Then you're left alone to fend for yourself. We should all have something to eat together."

"For one thing," I answered, amused at my own understanding, "when you hear that gentle whisper to your soul telling you to do something, there's no way you ought to even think about not doing it. Secondly, I'm not going to be alone for long. Clayton is coming by in a while to visit and have some tea. I'll be fine, so concentrate on your own family. I think this dinner could be just the thing you've been needing."

That teasing look came to Brian's face that I used to dread seeing when we were kids. It always meant he was going to pick on me for something. Usually something that would make me squirm with embarrassment.

"Clayton is coming over? Just the two of you alone in this big old house?"

"It's nothing," I answered, feeling my face flush with heat. "He's just concerned and wants to make sure I'm okay."

"Sure." Brian laughed. "That's why he always stares at you like a lovesick schoolboy. I think everyone has noticed it but you."

I was ready to hit him, but then Suzanne came outside with the boys. "I'll put in the order as soon as everyone decides what they want on their pizza," she said. "We're all pretty hungry. Even anchovies sound good, and I hate them."

"That's those fishy things, right, Mom?" Josh asked while wrinkling his freckled nose in disgust. "I don't want any. I won't eat a pizza with fish on top. I'd rather starve."

Brian stooped down to look at both boys. "Actually, I had a better idea for dinner. I was thinking of taking you two cowboys and your mother out to eat somewhere nice. That is, if you'd like to do that. If it's okay."

Suzanne looked shocked. "Well, what about Annie? She ought to come, too."

"I've got plans," I answered. "And I've got just enough time to take a hot bath and change clothes, so you guys had better get going."

Suzanne looked at me with a desperate expression. "But, I . . ."

I patted her shoulder. "Just go."

We all hugged and they piled in their car, then I watched as they drove down the road.

In the distance, I could hear the phone ringing inside the house. I dashed up the steps and through the door until the receiver was in my hand.

"Hello?" I panted. No question, I needed more exercise.

"Did I catch you at a bad time?" The sound of Clayton's voice surprised me.

"No, of course not. I was just seeing my brother and his family off. I had to run in from outside to catch the phone."

"I don't mean to disturb you. I just wanted to confirm our plans for tonight and make sure you're still up for sharing some tea."

"Yes," I blurted, hoping it didn't sound too eager. "I mean, if you are. I'd understand if you had a long day and just wanted to relax."

"You buried your beloved grandmother today, Annie," he

answered. "Your day was far more trying than mine. That's why I wanted to check and make sure you hadn't changed your mind. Is it still okay if I come by at seven?"

"Seven's perfect," I said, relieved he wasn't backing out. I was looking forward to his company more than I wanted to. "I'll have the kettle whistling by then."

"No doubt I'll hear it long before I pull into the driveway." He chuckled. "Velma's old teapot howls pretty loud when the water boils. I remember."

"It sure does." I laughed back. "I was amazed to find out she hadn't gotten a new one after all this time. That battered kettle has been around forever."

"Sometimes it's the old familiar things that mean the most. I think Velma liked it that way."

He spoke of her with such affection that it made me miss feeling admiration for her myself. I had always loved her like a mother. Her comforting arms were all I knew. Still, I couldn't get past the horror she caused by stealing my baby away.

"Annie? Are you still there?"

I cleared my throat to chase away the memories. "Yes. I'm here."

"Well, if seven is still okay I'll see you then, all right?"

"I'm looking forward to it," I answered. "Drive carefully."

Chapter 13

I hung up and started up the staircase to draw a bath when the phone rang again. My heart did a flip-flop thinking it was probably Clayton. Maybe he forgot to tell me something.

"Hello," I answered, waiting to hear his voice. Instead, what came through was my mother's.

"Annie, it's me. I hope you don't mind my calling."

Don't mind? Since when does it matter what I feel or need?

"It's fine. What can I do for you?"

There was a slight pocket of silence before she spoke. "I want to ask a favor of you. You and Brian both, actually. I don't deserve anything from either one of you, but you might say that something told me to ask anyway. I don't really have anything to lose."

Something told her to ask. There it was again. Didn't I just get done telling my own brother that when you get that voice in your soul telling you to do something that you should only do one thing and that is to do it?

"It's okay," I said back. "Go ahead and ask the favor."

"If you would rather not, just say so. I would certainly understand, but, well, I was hoping we could go to church this Sunday. Together. You, me, and Brian."

My breath caught in my throat. There was nothing that would keep me away from church this Sunday. It was the day I would see my little girl for the very first time. The day I thought would never come, thanks to a long-buried secret.

"Actually, I was planning on going. I don't know about Brian."

"Could you ask him for me? I think he would be more apt to accept if the idea came from you. I'm not sure after today how he feels about being around me."

"He feels like I do," I responded. "Hurt."

She waited and I heard her breathing. For some reason it brought tears to my eyes.

"I know you're both hurting. I'm hurting, too, Annie. Just because I was the one who walked away, it doesn't mean I was ever at peace with my decision. I hated who I was. I wanted to be a mother to my children, but I was too weak and too messed up. Drugs controlled my life. But you don't know how many times I'd wake up screaming in the night after having dreams that you and Brian were in trouble and I couldn't get to you. You don't know how many times I broke down just seeing a mother and her children in the grocery store or playing

67

in the park. I hurt, Annie. Maybe not the same as you and Brian, but I hurt very deeply just the same."

It was something I never pictured before. I was always too busy focusing on what Brian and I had gone through. It never occurred to me that our mother's choice to walk away put her through any kind of torment. I thought it was her decision, so it must've been what she wanted. Then again, didn't I do the same thing with Grandma Hatcher when I walked away and severed the ties? Sure, I had my reasons. I felt more than vindicated for such a bold move, but it hurt. Every day. It felt like a part of me was missing.

It hurt so much at times that I actually reached out to call her on the phone, but then my pride would hang up the receiver like an invisible hand. After all, I got pregnant and disappointed her. Just like the daughter that she was so ashamed of. If I wasn't good enough for Grandma Hatcher to love anymore even though I made a mistake, I'd leave. I'd move away and never look back again. I'd be doing a favor for the both of us.

But she did love me. I knew she did. I just couldn't convince myself of it because that empty spot that drove Brian to seek out affairs also made me feel unworthy. Unlovable. Unable to accept it because my own mother didn't love me.

Even when I did try and tell myself I was worthy and let down my guard long enough to let Michael into my heart, I regretted it like nothing before. It left me pregnant and alone. It was a lot safer just to remember that my own mother didn't care, so that must mean I wasn't worth it. The same cop-out as my brother was clinging to. It all suddenly became so clear.

I thumped a swallow and squeezed the phone to my ear. "We're all hurting. I think going to church together this Sunday would be a good first step. I'll talk to Brian and make sure he's there, too."

"Thank you, Annie. For what it's worth, I want you to know that I'm proud of the beautiful woman that you've become."

"Don't be proud of me," I blurted in reflex. The very thought of it was out of the question. She wouldn't say that if she knew the mess I made of my life.

"Why do you say that?"

"Because it's true."

"Because it's true or because you've convinced yourself it's true? No matter what mistakes we've made in our life, if we learn from them and turn them around for good, we can feel proud of who we are and how far we've come."

Wasn't that what Clayton had said to me earlier? It wasn't the trials that mattered, but what you did as a result of them? I thirsted for lessons such as this. If they were real, then it was life-changing.

Maybe there was a way to release all the darkness I carried and bask in the sun. A way to forgive others as well as myself. I knew I didn't want to continue the way I had been living for so long. I had a job I liked and a place of my own, but my past was always nipping like a frantic dog at my heels. I was always running from the person I was.

"I've heard that before," I finally answered. "That it's not the trials in our lives that matter, but the things we do as a result of them that counts."

"It's in God's word, Annie. All the answers are there if you seek them out. I've found that out when I was at my lowest low, and it literally saved my life. I see the damage I've caused to my children over my weak ways and I know I can't make it go away. But God can. With your help and acceptance of Him. I promise you that."

Promises from a woman who could never live up to them before? That should've been as meaningless as singing a song to the deaf, but I had the feeling the woman on the phone with me was hardly the same one who left us at Grandma Hatcher's doorstep. Something told me she was different. And that something, was it God?

"Well, we'll see you on Sunday," I said. "I'm glad you suggested it. It will be good for us."

"I'm so glad you feel that way," she replied. It sounded as if her voice was choked with emotion. "I'm so blessed to have any time with you that I can."

"Good-bye, then."

"Good-bye, Annie."

I hung up and drew a long sigh. Time together was something she carelessly threw away before, but now scrambled desperately to recapture. I began to wish I could do the same with Grandma Hatcher and pick up the phone, hear her voice, sit next to her in the church congregation. If only I had that chance to make up for the wrongs of the past. If only she could hear me.

"We've all done so wrong, Gram," I said as I stared at her vacant chair. "Not one person in this family is free of making choices that have hurt another person's life. What you did was wrong. I can't understand how you could've kept that secret from me all this time, but I'm not without fault. I pushed you out of my life and never allowed us to be close again.

"Maybe if I had, you would've been more apt to tell me. Maybe if I just stayed in Claxton with my family, you would've found the strength to tell me the truth before now.

"Then there's Brian, Gram. He's done so much to break Suzanne's heart and put the boys through so much pain. I don't know if they'll ever forgive him for it. I hope he hasn't lost the one thing he ever loved.

69

"Even your dear friend next door has made mistakes that hurt those she loved. She told me, Gram. She told me all about the rape and how she kept it from her daughter, only to drive her over the edge once she confessed her hidden secret. We've all made wrong choices and have caused such heartache. I'm sorry for my part. I truly am. I'm sorry that I walked out of this house where you raised me and never came back. I'm sorry that I forced you out of my life that way. Most of all, I'm sorry you died before I got the chance to tell you that I love you, Gram. I really do love you."

My legs grew weak as I sank down to the floor and buried my face in my hands. I cried from the deepest caverns of my heart, letting loose the pain that had housed itself there like a rock that never moved. How I wished I'd said those words earlier when Grandma Hatcher was here. When it would've made a difference. Before it was too late.

She heard you, Annie, and she's weeping along with you. It's not too late to forgive, not for either one of you, the voice said.

My crying stopped as I caught my breath. This time it wasn't a subtle whisper to my soul, but a distinct voice that came through loud and clear. The voice of hope when I needed to hear it the most. The voice of God leading the way.

"It's not too late," I repeated, smiling through my tears. Slowly, I got up and walked over to Gram's old chair. For the first time ever, I sat in it.

Chapter 14

The doorbell chimed shortly after seven o'clock. When I opened it, Clayton stood on the front step with a beautiful bouquet of flowers in his hands and a smile on his face.

"I hope you like tiger lilies," he said. "I couldn't resist them. They're nearly as breathtaking to look at as you are."

Heat crawled up my face as I took them and motioned him inside. "I love them. That was so sweet of you, Clayton. Thank you very much."

I put them in a vase with water and then poured two cups of tea. We sat at the kitchen table with nothing but quiet and time to talk.

"How are you holding up?" he asked, true concern in his gaze.

I shrugged. "I think I'm hanging in there. My mother called earlier and asked if Brian and I would go to church with her this Sunday. I think that will be a good place to start as far as piecing our relationship back together."

"I'm glad," he answered. "I know you must be very anxious to see Grace on Sunday, also. Have you prepared yourself for that and how you're going to handle it?"

"How can I possibly prepare myself to see my own daughter for the very first time? I know I can't run over and hold her like I long to. I can't stroke her hair and tell her I'm her mommy. It's going to kill me, but I know my boundaries. She's happy with the parents she has, and I know she has a better life than I could give her. Still, it's going to tear me apart to just stand at a distance and see her. You just have no idea how much I love her. Even though I thought she died at birth, I still loved my little girl with all of my heart for all of these lonely years."

He leaned forward and brushed my cheek with his finger. "I'll be there for you, Annie. I just hope you know that. I'll be right there if you need a shoulder to cry on or a hand to hold. Anything at all. I care about you, and my heart aches over what you have to deal with. I've been praying for you, and I know God will turn it all around for good."

I raised my gaze to meet his and saw such sincerity. It made me think back to when I told Michael I was pregnant with his child and he told me he'd do the right thing and marry me. He would have. I knew that. If anything, Michael always did what he said he would do, but it wasn't honest. It wasn't because he cared. He was going to stand by me because he felt like an animal caught in a trap. What Clayton was giving me was the real thing. The kind of caring that came from the heart. Something I always thought happened to other people, but not to me.

"That means a lot to me," I said, blinking back a rush of tears. "More than you know."

To my surprise, he stood up and walked over to where I was sitting. Gently, he took both of my hands and made me stand up, too. There had never been anything so right. I felt such a power working around us. When he drew me into his arms and gave me a tender kiss, it was as if I had been aimlessly roaming through life right up until then, but finally found my way home. Every part of me relaxed. There was no craziness, no losing control, no getting swept up in a careless flurry. Instead, we blended together as if it was simply meant to be.

He drew back and stared into my contented eyes. My lips still tingled from the thrill of his kiss. "You're the one He sent me. You're the woman God chose. I've prayed on that for so many years, and now I know that special once in a lifetime love I always longed for is right here in my arms."

Tears streamed down my face. "I feel it, too. Like our meeting and falling in love was a part of a destined plan. Instead of feeling unsure and scared, I feel joyous and at peace. Like I'm where I belong."

"Then you won't go back?" he asked, unwilling to release me from his embrace. "You'll stay in Claxton and give this a chance? You won't make me chase after you all the way to Columbus?"

My laughter flowed freely and felt like such medicine to my weary soul. "You would do that? Chase after me? This is beginning to sound like a kooky movie."

"Kooky or not, I'd do anything to make sure you don't get away. I wasn't kidding when I told you I've waited years for this. I knew God would send me my answer. I knew it was all on His time, and this is it. I knew it when I kissed you. Actually, I think I knew it the moment I laid eyes on you."

I pulled him closer and gave him a kiss. It led to another and then another. Finally, all I could manage to say was, "I owe God a really big thank you."

The doorbell sounded again, just as we were about to share another kiss. I took a deep breath and told Clayton I would be right back. He looked as disappointed to have an interruption as I was.

I opened the door to Edna, who held a large dish covered in foil. "I hope you don't mind my popping in on you like this. I knew today was a very difficult day for you and made one of my spinach lasagnas in case you were too tired to deal with dinner. I would've gotten it over here sooner, but I was out of ricotta cheese and had to make a trip to the market. It kind of slowed things down a bit. I also noticed that Clayton's car is here. Is everything all right?"

He walked up behind me. "In fact, everything is fine. Annie and

I were just having some tea and talking. Would you like to join us, Gram?"

She eyed us both as if she saw something we didn't. Her grin was a bit sinister. "Well, I don't want to intrude on whatever may be happening between you. It shows, you know. You both are kind of glowing."

One of the things I loved about Edna was her bluntness, but I wasn't sure if she was mistaken or not. Nothing was really happening. We were simply kissing, that's all. Nothing out of control. It was probably just a passing thing.

Don't kid yourself, Annie, this is once in a lifetime! my mind told me.

I took the lasagna and ushered Edna in. "You aren't intruding, for heaven's sakes. Come in. Have some tea with us. I know today was rough for you, too."

She came in and followed us back to the kitchen. Clayton got another cup and poured her some tea. All the while, she kept watching us both with a funny kind of fascination. I wanted to ask her what it was she was staring at, but at the moment, I was afraid of her answer.

"The service went very well," I finally said, taking my seat. "I think Grandma Hatcher would've been very pleased."

Edna nodded, looping her shaking finger through the handle on her cup. "She had a lot of people who cared about her. It was a very touching farewell. I also noticed Mrs. Richards introducing herself to you. How did that go?"

"It went better than I expected," I answered. "She is a very lovely woman. Very strong and together. I wasn't sure how meeting me would make her feel, but I didn't pick up any negative feelings whatsoever. In fact, she was very warm toward me. She said that Grace will be at church this Sunday and I'll be able to see her then. I told her I had no intentions of upsetting her or telling her who I am. She understood that I just want to see her. Be near her. The rest will be ironed out later."

Clayton sipped his tea, which must have been as lukewarm as mine. "Lola Richards is an extraordinary woman. She is the kind of person who would open her home to you, give you anything you need, without question. Her husband, Paul, is the same way. He actually fixed twenty used bikes last Christmas, repainted them, and put big ribbons on them to give to needy kids in this community."

"They sound ideal for Grace," I answered, a hint of sadness in my voice. "I'm so thankful she has parents like that. It's the best outcome I could've asked for."

Edna sipped her tea with a thoughtful look. Her hand tremored badly as she put the cup back down. "I don't know about that," she said, mopping up what she spilled with her napkin. "That may be a very comforting outcome, but certainly not the best. The best would be if you could also be a part of Grace's life. I'm not so sure keeping your identity a secret and having you admire her from afar is the right way to handle this. It seems something better could be arranged."

"I agree," Clayton said. "I've been thinking a lot about that, myself. It's a delicate situation, for sure. Grace is very happy and I know the Richardses love her very much. But, you are her biological mother, Annie. You didn't give her up. You didn't even know she was alive. It doesn't seem right that you can't have any kind of connection to her."

"Believe me," I said, tears welling in my eyes, "I would love nothing more than to be able to let her know who I am, get close to her, share in her life somehow. But I can't do that. Not when the life she has is so stable and loving. What do I have to offer her compared to what she has right now?"

"Something no one else has," Edna commented. "The love of her real birth mother."

It made me smile as tears ran down my cheeks. "God knows, I do love her. So very much."

"God does know," Clayton answered. "He'll work in this situation and make it right. I believe He wants Grace to have all of you in her life. Maybe we ought to just turn it over to Him and see what He comes up with."

"Of course, it would be nice if you lived here again," Edna said. "Not just for Grace, but for your brother and his family. And, well, for my grandson. There I said it."

Clayton laughed and raised his brows in surprise. "That's a bit pushy, don't you think, Gram? If you don't watch out, you're going to scare this poor beautiful young lady off and then I won't stand a chance with her."

Edna smiled and patted my arm. Those clear eyes sparkled as brilliantly as tiny gemstones. "I don't think this girl is going to get away that easily, Clayton. Not if she knows what's good for her."

Chapter 15

Sunday morning was filled with promise. The sky was clear and a brilliant blue, and the air pleasantly crisp and cool. But it wasn't the fall temperatures that made me shiver as Brian and I walked into the sanctuary. It was knowing my little girl was there. The child I still carried in my heart. The daughter I gave birth to and never got the chance to hold. My eyes eagerly searched the congregation as my mother spotted us and came over.

"I'm so glad you both came," she said, smiling. "After how things went between us last time, I think this will be a better way to get acquainted. In God's house, hurts and anger somehow feel comforted and forgiven."

Brian smiled softly. "I agree. I think this is a good place to sort everything out. Not just with you, Mom, but within myself. A lot of the anger I unleashed on you in your hotel room was anger I feel toward myself. I'm beginning to see how no matter what has happened to you in your past, it's still your choice how you deal with it. I don't want to be the kind of husband and father who runs scared to another woman. I love my wife and my boys more than life itself. In fact, I've left the woman I was living with and have taken a temporary apartment ten minutes from our house. This will give me a chance to slowly get closer to the boys and to Suzanne. I think we can really make it work. We even talked about attending church together—as a family. Suzanne said she would think about it."

"Oh, Brian," I said, wrapping my arms around him. "You don't know how happy I am to hear that."

Our mother put her arms around us both. "I'm proud of you, Brian. And of you, Annie. I see two very special people with a lot of hurt in the past, but who have strong hearts and a will to survive. We can't go back and correct all that went wrong, but the future is a gift. It's ours to unwrap and to cherish. We can make it whatever we want it to be with forgiveness and faith in God, and if we have each other."

Just then, the choir assembled at the altar and the service was about to begin. We spotted Edna in the third pew, and she invited us to sit with her. I introduced her to our mother and they warmly embraced. She patted me on the knee with a gleam in her eye, as if to say she was pleased at where things were going. Clayton came out and everyone stood as the church filled up with song.

I kept looking over my shoulder, hoping to see Mrs. Richards and her husband. To know they were at least there. That Grace was in Sunday school and I could soon see her. I kept wondering what she looked like. What her voice sounded like. How she smiled. My heart sank when I didn't see them. I began to fear that they backed out at the last minute. Maybe they weren't comfortable with the fact that I wanted to see my daughter. Maybe they didn't trust that I wouldn't cause her any harm. I thought I had put Mrs. Richards' mind to rest about that, but perhaps she wasn't as convinced as she seemed.

I couldn't blame her, really. Grace was her child now. Her life. Even if she wasn't of her own flesh and blood. I'm sure it didn't make her love Grace any less. Having me in the picture now must be quite unsettling. Maybe they began to fear that Grace would end up in the middle, being tugged back and forth between two needy mothers who refused to give her up. As much as I wanted to claim my own daughter, I knew it was too late. I had to stay out of her life. It would be kinder for her that way. She probably hadn't even been told she was adopted. It would totally crumble her world. I took one last look behind me, but Mr. and Mrs. Richards were nowhere in sight. Edna must've sensed my tension and gathered my hand in hers.

"Give it up to God," she whispered. "That's all you can do. If it's meant to work out like you want, then it will."

After several hymns, we all sat back down as Clayton took to the podium and greeted everyone in the sanctuary. He explained that this was to be a very memorable morning. That he had a very special message to deliver.

"Luke 17:3 gives us a very powerful verse to ponder. It says, take heed to yourselves: if thy brother trespass against thee, rebuke him; and if he repent, forgive him." His gaze scanned everyone's faces. He smiled when he settled on mine. "Not an easy thing. I don't know any one of us sitting here today who hasn't been hurt by someone's actions and had their lives affected in some way. It's impossible to love without disappointing. Man will always let you down, therefore we are constantly wounded and scarred by those we care about. It's a fact of life. There is no perfect trust or perfect love between those of us in the flesh. We are born sinners. We are always falling short of who we want to be or who others expect us to be.

"Though, good intentions we may have, we hurt people by our selfish ways or by lies or by breaking trust that was supposed to be foolproof. It happens in marriages all the time. In families and friendships. They crumble because of failed expectations. But, what God wants to show us through His word is that there is a freedom from the hurt each one of us carries. A cleansing of the wrongs in the past. It is called forgiveness. Just as Jesus did on the cross. Forgiveness. It sets the suffering free."

My mother leaned forward and whispered to Brian and me. "I think this sermon was written just for us. God always knows what we need to hear and when we need to hear it."

Brian nodded and smiled. I did the same. It did seem rather uncanny. Every word that Clayton was saying I thirsted to hear.

There was a quiet commotion to our left as Suzanne and the boys arrived. Brian was pleasantly surprised and moved over so they could sit together. I could see the healing already taking place in their family. Suzanne reached out and held on to her husband's hand as he introduced his family to our mother. The boys kept tugging on their stiff dress shirt collars, but politely smiled and greeted their new grandmother, then went back to fidgeting in their seats.

"You may say, 'But Pastor, I can't forgive. It makes me weak. It tells the person who hurt me that it's okay what they did. I can try to forget it, but I really don't think that I can.'" Clayton paused and let those words sink in. "But what are you left with if you don't forgive other people? A burdened heart. A bitter soul. Wounds that never heal. That will be your solemn fate, my friends. Because, you see, forgiving those that hurt you is not a weakness. It does not make what happened okay. It doesn't mean you have to forget. Forgiving is a gift that you give to yourself so that you can be healed from the past, free to live again, and be joyful."

The doors to the back of the church opened. People turned and looked to see who had come in. I turned around, as well. My heart leaped when I saw it was Mr. and Mrs. Richards. Walking between them and holding both of their hands was a beautiful little girl with long hair and wearing a pastel pink dress, white tights, and black buckled shoes. She was shyly looking at all the people and smiled at certain ones that she obviously knew. I was breathless. My eyes couldn't leave her.

I expected them to settle into an empty pew, but instead they continued to walk down the aisle and joined Clayton up front at the pulpit. Brian and I looked at one another with shock on both of our faces. Edna mumbled a thank you to God and leaned against me, patting my leg. All I could do was sit as motionless as a statue. My baby was real and right in front of me.

Clayton smiled at Mr. and Mrs. Richards. He then gave a playful wink to Grace. "Right on time. Praise Jesus." His anxious gaze darted to me. "We have a little surprise planned today. A reunion, of sorts. One that none other than God could have arranged. We're all very blessed to share in this special moment. I'll let Mr. and Mrs. Richards tell you the story."

Mrs. Richards stooped down and gave Grace a kiss before taking the podium and facing the congregation. She was poised and lovely in an ivory skirt suit and seemed very comfortable being up in front of people. She smiled at everyone and said hello before casting me a glance. Once we locked eyes, she drew a deep breath and began her prepared speech.

"When Pastor told me the message was going to be about forgiveness today, it made me think long and hard about how important that is. Not only for those who have been hurt by others, but for those who have need to forgive themselves. If my husband and I hadn't decided to stand up here before you today and do what we are about to do, we would be struggling to forgive ourselves for the rest of our lives. Instead, we want to do what is right. What the Lord has told us to do. We want to trust in His plan and come forward."

At that point, Mr. Richards joined her at the podium with Grace in tow. She toyed with her long hair as her daddy slid in and shared the microphone. "My wife and I were very blessed years ago when we adopted little Grace. As you all knew, we had never been able to conceive a child and wanted to be parents very, very much. We prayed on it and prayed on it until one day we got our answer. The adoption agency had a baby for us. A brand-new little girl."

I leaned against Edna who was squeezing my hand. Brian placed an arm around me from the other side. All I could do was stare at the child I thought I had cast to the wind that morbid day. She was everything I dreamed she would be. She was absolutely perfect.

Mr. Richards looked back down at Grace. They smiled at each other. "Until just recently, we never knew the birth mother's identity. We only knew she was quite young and couldn't give her child a life. It seemed like the answer to our prayers."

A pause followed as Mrs. Richards took over. "And it was. We had our little girl and life was simply perfect, but my husband and I never forgot about Grace's birth mother. We wondered about her. Prayed she was safe and well. We often asked God to somehow thank her for the courageous thing she did—giving her own baby up to strangers. We knew what a loving and selfless thing that was. We knew she must be a very special woman. It didn't seem likely we would ever be able to meet her, but God has His ways. What is meant to happen, happens. Well, I guess what I'm trying to say is, you all have watched Grace grow up right before your very eyes. We've brought her to church since she was a baby. You're all her extended family. I think you will all share in this joyous announcement we have today. Grace can finally be reunited with her natural birth mother. God has brought the two of them together."

There were gasps and murmurs as I clapped a hand over my mouth and felt myself begin to shake. This was impossible. I told Mrs. Richards that I wouldn't take Grace away from them. They were the only parents she'd ever known. I didn't want to disrupt the life they had built and her happy home. Her security. What was she doing? How was Grace going to react? I held back my sobs as Clayton smiled back at me.

Grace seemed so calm. She fidgeted with her dress and then looked out at the people that were staring at her. I thought this would pull the rug right out from under her, but instead, she seemed amazingly grounded.

My mother saw my reaction and became instantly lost. "What is it, Annie? What's going on?"

I kept my eyes pinned to the little girl standing up on the altar. "That's my baby, Mom. That beautiful child is your granddaughter."

Mrs. Richards saw me weeping and gave me a caring smile. "You see, we always told Grace that she was a special child. That she was adopted, which meant she had a mommy out there somewhere who loved her very much, but couldn't keep her. Every night when she said her prayers, before she fell asleep, she'd bless all the people she held dear in her heart. Her mommy and daddy, her grandparents, her playmates and friends, Pastor, her Sunday school class here at church, and last, without fail, she'd always ask God to bless her real mommy—and to give her a hug since Grace was unable to. Today, she will get that chance."

Just then, Grace stepped forward. Mr. Richard had to hoist her up in his arms so she could lean into the microphone and speak. When I heard her voice, I couldn't control my sobs any longer. I had to let them go.

"I always prayed I'd get the chance to meet my real mommy." She scanned the audience with beautiful eyes. "Would you please come up here so I can hug you? I've been waiting a really long time."

I couldn't move. It was too good to be true. My daughter knew of me, prayed for me, and carried me in her heart. She actually wanted to hug me! Brian and Edna kept telling me to get up, and they pulled on my arms. Everything was rubbery and unwilling to function. Then Clayton stepped down from the pulpit and extended his hand to me. It was the strength I needed to draw from. I rose up from my seat and walked with him to the steps of the altar. His face was beaming as he led me up to where my daughter was waiting. I hardly dared to breathe.

"Grace," he said. "This is your birth mother. Her name is Annie and she's a very special lady. She's been waiting a very long time to meet you. I think that hug that you just mentioned is something she needs more than anything else in the world."

All I could do was crumble to my knees and take her into my arms. She was so delicate and beautiful. I could've held her forever. I loved the sweet sunshine smell of her hair. The feel of her small arms embracing me. The soft satin of her cheek pressed against mine. All the lost years didn't seem to matter anymore. The here and now was quite spectacular enough, and I wanted to keep it forever.

"Oh, Grace," I said. "You're so grown up and pretty. I've always loved you and thought about you every day. All I ever wanted was to hold you like this. Thank you, God. Thank you for making it happen."

She backed out of my arms and wiped my tears with her fingers. "Don't cry. This is supposed to be a happy day. Now we can love each other forever. My mommy and daddy said it was okay. I asked if I could have you for a mommy, too. You'll like that, won't you? We could kind of be like a great big giant family."

At a loss, I stood and looked at Mr. and Mrs. Richards, who were huddling together and shedding tears of their own.

"I don't understand," I said to them. "What exactly does this mean?"

Mrs. Richards came up and dotted Grace's nose with her finger. She then took my hand and held it tight. "Once my husband and I realized the situation of this adoption and the real identity of Grace's birth mother, we realized that not telling Grace who you were wasn't the right way to handle this. It would be too explosive a secret. Secrets can lay dormant, but sooner or later, they become exposed. We didn't want to risk hurting Grace by deception, even if we felt it was for her own protection. It would've been out of love and out of good intentions, but it still would've been wrong. She has the right to know about you, just as you have the right to know her. Neither of you deserve to miss out on what God intended in the first place."

I absorbed everything she was saying and kept thinking of Grandma Hatcher. She did give in to the temptation of deception to protect me and spare me from what she thought would be too much for me to handle. It hurt. It stole my daughter away from me. It devastated me in ways I'd never forget. What a blessing that my little girl's adoptive parents wouldn't let Grace get hurt that way. They were wise enough not to give in to their temptation and stepped forward with the truth.

Would I have been as strong if I were them? I wondered. Would I have been any better than Grandma Hatcher?

I could almost understand, now that I had Grace by my side, how someone could want to protect their child so badly that they lose their sense of reason. Feeling how my heart was overflowing for my little girl, I knew I'd do anything for her. Now and always. Even if I made mistakes, it was because I loved her so much. I could finally see it. More importantly, I could finally forgive. Grandma Hatcher loved me and only wanted the best for me, even if she did make a horrible mistake.

"I never wanted to take her away from you," I said softly. "She's happy. She has a loving home. I'm single and don't have much to offer."

Mrs. Richards smiled. "Oh, but you do. More than you realize. In fact, my husband and I have discussed it and we want Grace to have you in her life. If it's okay with you, I think we can work this out where she won't have to lose either one of us. Clayton told us that you might be staying in Claxton. We really hope you do. That way, we can work this out where Grace can have all of us in her life. Perhaps stay where she is since she knows that as home, but spends weekends with you. Do things with you, get to know you, and you can catch up on the lost years. I truly believe God has worked powerfully in this situation and brought us together to be a nice, big family. We hope you feel that way, too."

Clayton came by me and held my hand. I could barely contain my tears. "You have no idea how perfect that sounds. How can I ever thank you?"

"By taking us all out for a giant ice cream sundae," Grace chimed, tugging on my hemline. "I like mine with a lot of whipped cream and I always ask for an extra cherry!"

Everyone laughed and the congregation burst into applause. It was the most perfect moment of my life. After so many years of running away from the home and family that I left behind, I was finally back to stay. The very thing that tore my life apart when I first got here was the miracle that made it all fit together. And I learned a wealth about life and love that I never knew before. About the power of truth and the miracle of forgiving. About how to start over again. I gazed into Clayton's eyes and knew this was my wonderful beginning. I also knew without a doubt that he was part of my plan.

"May I say something?" I asked him, gesturing toward the microphone.

"Of course," he answered, escorting me there. "Take all the time that you need."

I looked out at all the faces smiling back at me, most were moist with tears of joy. Edna almost made me laugh out loud because she grinned and clapped before giving me an enthusiastic thumbs up. My mother swiped her eyes and beamed with joy. How I loved this church and all the people here. I drank in all the love that was around me. The kind of love that makes a place a home. That makes you know where you belong.

"I came back to Claxton hoping to have time with my grandmother once I learned she was so very ill. It had been years since I had seen her. Years since I made any attempt to talk with her at all. I thought I'd have time to make up for that. When I got here, she had already passed away. She died with our foolish pride still making a wall between us. Instead of that wall breaking down in memory of her passing, it got bigger and taller. It got impossible to climb because I learned that she had a secret. The secret was my baby. My precious little girl. I thought she had died at birth, but my grandmother turned her over for adoption. She was afraid because I was so very young. She didn't want me to not have a chance in life because I had too heavy a load to carry." I looked at my mother and saw her dabbing her eyes. My story was hitting a nerve within her. "She kept it to herself all of these years and her only dying wish was for me to know the truth."

Instinctively, Grace knew I was hurting. She whispered something in her mother's ear and then came over to tug on my hand.

"She'd be happy now," she said, looking up at me with a smile. "She'd be real happy from heaven to see us all together today."

Her insight and her warm, caring heart amazed me. I picked her up and held her tight. "Yes, she would. And I know she's watching this, which is why I wanted to say something to her." I kissed the velvet softness of my daughter's cheek and then wept as I looked up toward the heavens. "Grandma Hatcher, I love you with all of my heart and I want you to know that I do forgive you. You loved me the way I love this sweet angel I'm holding in my arms. And when you love that strongly, sometimes you go too far to protect them and end up hurting people. I know you're listening, Grandma Hatcher. I know you're here with us today, and I thank you for sharing your secret and undoing the wrong that was done years ago. If it wasn't for your courage to do that, I would've missed out on this moment." I smiled at Grace and then looked out at the congregation. "This is all I've ever dreamed of."

Everyone stood and applauded as Grace and I hugged. The Richardses came over and joined in. That was when Clayton took over the microphone and we all went back to sit down.

He leaned against the podium, smiling broadly at my new family as we filled in the first pew. Brian and Suzanne were bursting to come over, as well as my mother and Edna, but they waited while Clayton ended his message.

"I couldn't have given you any more of a powerful example of God's forgiveness if I read it straight from the scriptures. Because the past has been let go, because the wrongs against us have been washed clean, because He has given us the gift of being born again if we repent our sins, there is a miracle in Claxton. A new family has been born. A little girl who has been loved all of her life, now has even more love to hold. A tragic secret that tainted Velma's soul is set free. It is erased. It is forgiven because with God as our Lord and Savior, it is our promise that if we repent and love Him with all of our souls, the suffering will end. The hurts will heal. There will be peace once more. Because of that gift, Annie is reunited with her beautiful daughter. Because of that gift, the pain of the past if now set free. Each and every one of you who have a wound to heal, you've seen the power right here before your eyes. You watched as a terrible wrong was made right.

"I urge you to also find it in your hearts to forgive the ones who have hurt you. No matter how hard, no matter how much you may have to struggle to release the pain, do it for yourself. For your life. For the God that has great plans for you if you only follow His word, and His word is to forgive thine enemies. Love thine enemies and your reward shall be great." He pointed out to where I was sitting with my daughter, holding her hand tightly in mine. "We know His promise is true. He rewarded these wonderful people. Won't you also forgive and set yourself free? Won't you see what God has in store for you?"

We closed with a prayer and then the service ended. As the choir sang, people came over to congratulate me, Grace, and Mr. and Mrs. Richards. Grace adored all the attention and even loved meeting her new grandmother, her Aunt Suzanne, Uncle Brian, and cousins, Trevor and Josh. They were close to the same age and had a lot of things in common. Already, they had plans to play football together. I noticed Brian and Suzanne were smiling brightly and holding hands again. My brother had put his wedding ring back on and they looked like the couple they once were. Forgiving was setting their hurts free, as well. Their family was finally healing.

"You were pretty powerful up there," Clayton quietly commented, as he came up and slid his arm around me. "You would make a good Pastor's wife, you know. I think this congregation loved you!"

I blinked back in shock. "Was that a proposal?"

He let loose with that crazy, crooked smile. "Let's talk about it over a great big ice cream sundae. I think Grace had a really good idea."

"Hurray!" she cried, bouncing up and down. "Can my mom and dad come, too?"

"Let's all go," Clayton said, inviting Mr. and Mrs. Richards, Brian's family, my mother, and Edna, too. "I think we should make this one great big celebration!"

Then Grace got a worried look and drew everyone's attention. "That's a lot of sundaes and a lot of cherries, I think. What if they don't have enough to give me an extra one like I always have on mine?"

I giggled and gave the answer that I had waited so long for and felt so right in my heart. "I'll share mine with you because I love you so much. After all, that's what family is for!"

THE END

83

www.ingramcontent.com/pod-product-compliance
Lightning Source LLC
Chambersburg PA
CBHW070534130626
46555CB00003B/1412